The NOT-SO-UNIFORM Life of HOLLY-Mei

The NOT-SO-UNIFORM Life of HOLLY-Mei

CHRISTINA MATULA

inkyard PRESS

Recycling programs
for this product may
not exist in your area.

ISBN-13: 978-1-335-42488-4

The Not-So-Uniform Life of Holly-Mei

For questions and comments about the quality of this book, please contact us at CustomerService@Harlequin.com.

Inkyard Press
22 Adelaide St. West, 41st Floor
Toronto, Ontario M5H 4E3, Canada
www.InkyardPress.com

Printed in U.S.A.

To the city of Hong Kong 香港.
My home for fourteen years.

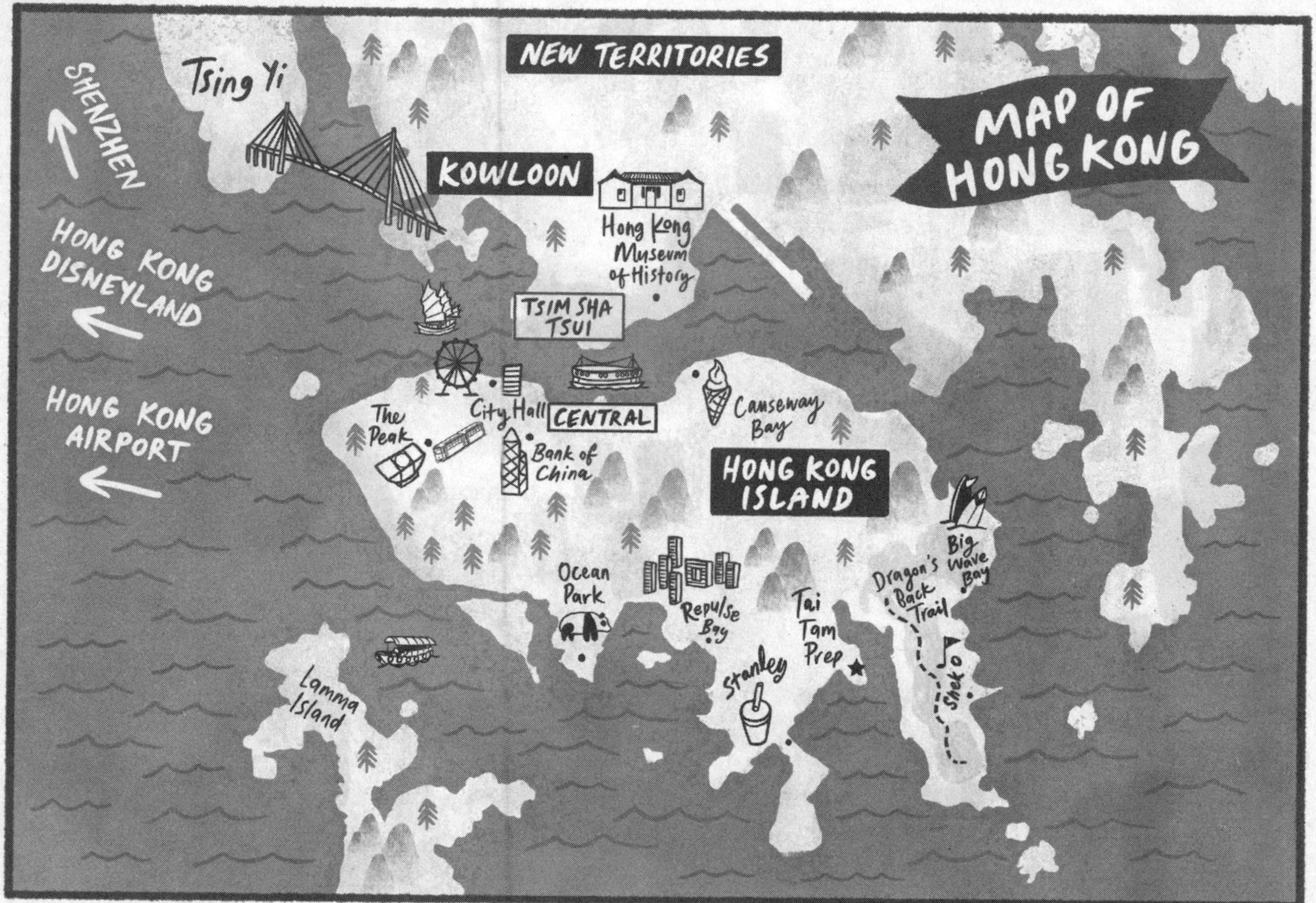
MAP OF HONG KONG
NEW TERRITORIES
Tsing Yi
SHENZHEN
KOWLOON
Hong Kong Museum of History
HONG KONG DISNEYLAND
TSIM SHA TSUI
HONG KONG AIRPORT
City Hall
CENTRAL
Causeway Bay
The Peak
Bank of China
HONG KONG ISLAND
Big Wave Bay
Dragon's Back Trail
Ocean Park
Repulse Bay
Tai Tam Prep
Shek O
Stanley
Lamma Island

1

Somewhere out in the world there must be kids who don't mind eating lunch alone. But not here, not me. I wrap my fingers tightly around my glass container, grip my book with the other hand, and step into the cafeteria of Maple Grove Elementary. The summer-school session is buzzing with freshly finished Grade 6 kids. I'm doing a mixed STEM/field hockey camp with girls from my school team. At the center of the room, Natalie, Katie, and Ellie are sitting together at a table. Their laughter and chatter float my way. I pause and try to catch a word or two, but I can't make anything out. I hold my head high and walk toward them. I don't want to spend another day by myself, with only the characters in my book as friends. My eyes drift to the empty seat at the table, my usual seat. Or it was until the middle of last month. But I have a plan that's going to solve everything. In the glass container are chocolate cupcakes that Millie, my younger sister, helped me make. She loves baking.

"Um, hi," I say with more confidence than I feel. I push the cupcakes toward them, like a peace offering.

Katie arches her eyebrows, like she's asking me a question.

"I brought some cupcakes. Double chocolate."

"Thanks," Natalie says. Our eyes meet, and I smile. I see her lips start to move upward like she's going to smile back.

"But no, thanks." Ellie interrupts us, her hand on her hip.

I look down at the buttercream frosting and the rainbow sprinkles. Who could say no to amazing cupcakes? Millie and I stayed up late to decorate them. I don't understand why they aren't inviting me back to sit at the lunch table. "Look, I've already apologized about the pizza party like, a million times," I say, my arms out, as if I could capture that quantity within their span.

The class pizza party. I cringe when I think about it. It all happened the last week of school when we were writing our final math test of the year, and the teacher, Ms. Takacs, left the room to take an emergency call. As soon as the door shut behind her, Logan Lucas yelled out, "Hey, what's the answer to question three?" It was multiple-choice, and someone yelled out, "C." Then he asked about question seven, and then about question nine. People were laughing and sharing their answers. I said, "Stop it. That's cheating!" But they continued until the teacher returned. A couple of days later when we got our marked tests back, I couldn't believe that lazy Logan Lucas, the boy who laughed at kids who liked to study, not only got the same mark as me, 90 percent, but was also told by Ms. Takacs, "That's a great improvement. I told you you'd do well if you applied yourself." When the rest of the class cheered Logan on, I just blurted it out. "Or maybe he had help." I didn't mean to; it just popped into my head and out of my mouth, like a runaway speech bubble. But Ms. Takacs heard, and not only did the whole class get detention, she also canceled our end-of-year pizza party.

"This isn't just about the pizza party," Natalie says gently.

I must have a confused look on my face, because Katie feels the need to explain. "Duh, you cost us the field hockey game yesterday, Holly-Mei Jones."

"We tied," I say.

"Yes, but we would have won if you didn't open your big mouth," Katie says.

"Again—" Ellie chimes in. "We're at this summer camp to become better players. Winners, not almost-winners."

"Hey, the ball hit my foot before going in the net," I say. In the game yesterday against a visiting top club from Ottawa, I received the pass from Ellie, but it bobbled and touched my foot as I took my shot. Even though the ball made that glorious *thump* sound when it hit the backboard of the goal, I knew it wasn't a goal, not a real goal, anyway. You can do a lot with the ball in a field hockey game, but it can never, ever touch your foot. It's the number one rule.

"But you didn't have to tell the umpire that. She

didn't see, so she would've let us keep the goal," says Katie.

Ellie looks at me and narrows her eyes. "And we would've won 1–0."

"But that wouldn't have been fair," I say. I broke the rule. There are consequences to breaking rules. There always are, or there always should be.

"Not fair to who?" asks Ellie. I look at her and mouth *whom*, but she doesn't notice and continues. "What's not fair is you snitching."

"A foul is a foul. It was the right thing to do," I say.

"Jeez, Holly-Mei. Why do you always have to be so *fair*?" Natalie says the word *fair* like it's a bad thing, and she throws her arms in the air, as if she's tired of explaining this to me, but I have no idea what she's talking about. "You always have to be right, do the right thing—"

Of course, I think.

"—even if it hurts others." She shakes her head and looks at me like she feels sorry for me, like I can't understand. But what I can't understand is why people don't feel strongly like I do about following rules. My mom always likes to remind us that rules help make the world good and fair. I sometimes watch the news with my dad, so I know that the world is not always a nice place, so why wouldn't I do my part to make it better?

"It's just a stupid field hockey game," I say.

Ellie says, "I'll tell you what's stupid—"

"Stop it." Natalie snaps at her. She turns to me and speaks in a gentle tone. "Holly-Mei, can't you just try to be more flexible? Think a little more about people's feelings?"

"Like how you thought about my feelings when you dropped me off the class chat?" I stare at her for a full second before I grab the box of cupcakes and march out of the cafeteria. I don't want them to see the tears that are on the verge of rolling down my face. Or think that I'm sorry for what I did, because I'm not. I'm only sorry that I lost my best friend.

As I bike home after camp, the sound of the leaves rustling and the black-capped chickadees singing help to cheer me up. I can't actually see the birds as I whiz by, but the male birds have this telltale whistling noise, *fee bee*, that I sometimes hear in our backyard. We have a bird feeder, and Dad keeps a video journal of all the birds he sees, and every weekend he proudly shows it to me and

Millie, and he even tries to teach us the bird sounds. Dad says chickadees are called tits back in England, where he's from, but Mom says he's not supposed to call them that here in Canada.

Our neighborhood is famous for its big old maple trees—their leaves turn the prettiest bright yellow, orange, and red in the autumn. That's why it's called Maple Grove. I love my street: in the spring, we have a huge block party after the snow finally melts, and in October the Halloween decorations are the scariest and treats the tastiest. Another house on the street has construction fencing around it, a sure sign that the new owners are going to build what Mom calls a *McMansion*. When our next-door neighbors retired, they sold their house—a bungalow, which looked almost like ours—and moved out west to be closer to their grandkids. The new owners not only tore the house down but they cut down all the maple trees in the backyard and put in a giant pool. Dad says fewer birds come to visit us now.

I jump off my bike and rest it against the side of our redbrick house. Despite the tall fence, I can hear the shrieking, laughing, and splashing of the neighbors' teenage girls and their friends in the swimming pool.

I kick off my shoes in the front hall and drop my bag on the floor, but after a couple of steps, I stop and look back at it, crumpled in the corner. I pick it up and take the cupcake container out and put the bag away in my room before Dad has a go at me later for being messy.

In the kitchen, I dump the contents of the container in the garbage can. The cupcakes are all broken and the frosting smushed, anyway. "Stupid cupcakes. Stupid friends," I mumble.

"Hi, honey," Mom says as she walks in.

I whip around. I'm surprised to see her. She's never home before seven o'clock, and it's barely gone three thirty.

"You're home from work early," I say, glancing around to make sure there's no hint of chocolate crumbs on the counter.

"I'm working from home this afternoon. And don't eat too much," she says, eyeing the empty cupcake container. "We're going out for dinner, to Yangtze."

Yangtze is our favorite Chinese restaurant. We go there whenever we have a birthday or some sort of celebration. My eyes widen, and my mouth starts to water thinking about all the delectable dishes we'll get to eat.

"What are we celebrating?" I ask.

Mom opens her mouth like she's going to say something, but instead smiles and says, "You'll see."

Her phone rings before I can ask more questions. I open the freezer and let the cool air and wispy condensation clouds waft over me before I grab a homemade Popsicle, or *ice lolly* as Dad calls them. I offer one to Mom, but she waves me off with a smile and mouths *Later* as she takes her call in the living room. This batch of Popsicles is creamy red bean, made with red bean paste and condensed milk, like a Chinese Creamsicle, one of Millie's culinary experiments. These are much nicer than her attempt at bubble tea Popsicles with homemade pearls, which left a sticky, flour-filled trail around the kitchen for days.

The screen door to the back patio is open, and the laughter from next door floats in. It's a sound that would normally be heard in our kitchen when Natalie and I would make grilled cheese sandwiches and do our homework together or just hang out. I shut my eyes tight and try not to think of school and what a nightmare Grade 7 might be in September. Will I be sitting alone at recess or, worse, hanging with Millie and her Grade 6 classmates? Will I have to spend my lunch hour alone, hiding behind a book?

"Baobei," Ah-ma says, *my treasure*, "everything okay?"

"I'm fine, meiyou wenti," I say, *no problem*.

Ah-ma strokes my hair. She is my Taiwanese grand-mother, my mom's mom. Her short silver hair looks freshly curled, and her soft round face crinkles at the edges when she smiles. She kisses me on the head and moves to the sink to fill the kettle. She reaches on tiptoe for her tin of pu'er tea, and when she opens it, it smells like a forest that doesn't get much sunlight. She puts a scoop in her favor-ite mug, the one decorated with a neon-pink *#1 Grandma* that Millie and I gave her for Christmas years ago.

"Ah-ma, what's this dinner all about?"

"Be patient, my love. Your mama has news." She smiles reassuringly at me.

Mom works long hours and travels a lot, and even though Dad is home more, he's often holed up in his study, especially when he can hear the rumblings of an ar-gument brewing over homework or the TV remote. Mom jokes that Dad is *so British* and likes to avoid confronta-tion. My mother, on the other hand, has no issue telling me exactly what she thinks about me and what I'm doing at any given time. Ah-ma is always there for me and my sister, though. She's lived with us since I was little, after my grandfather died. She was there for my first bike ride

with no training wheels (including the bandages that followed), my first bra, and my first period. And she makes
the best dumplings ever.

"I'll try a bit now," Mom says as she puts her phone
down and takes a bite of my Popsicle. "Pretty good." She
sits down beside me and touches my shoulder. "Honey,
Ah-ma tells me that Natalie hasn't been over in a few
weeks. Are you girls still in a little drama?"

My shoulders tense. This is not some *little drama*. This
is me losing my closest friend in the entire world. This
coming school year, Grade 7 is supposed to be our best
year yet, when we'll be the oldest and coolest kids in the
school. I'm going to be utterly lost without her.

"No, everything's fine," I say, forcing a smile. I want
to say something, but I don't want to worry her. Or disappoint her when she hears how it happened. I can tell
she gets a little annoyed when I blurt things out because
she'll say things like "Filter your thoughts" or "Think before you speak," which I try to do. But sometimes it's hard.
Mom says learning to master social skills is like any other
subject at school—I'm good at math, but Millie finds it
hard—so we both just need to practice more.

She pats my arm. "Tomorrow morning, why don't we

all bike over to the farmers market. Cherries are in season. I know you love those."

"Sure, Mom. That'll be nice."

"And there's a new exhibit at the science museum opening this weekend. Let's check it out on Sunday."

"Sounds good," I say, thankful that I'll be busy and not have to think about what anyone else is doing.

Six o'clock rolls around and all five of us pile into our Toyota RAV4 to head down Yonge Street to Yangtze. I sit in the middle seat in the back, between Ah-ma and Millie, even though Millie should be sitting here because she's the smallest, but she called *shotgun*, even though I don't even think that's a thing in the back of the car. Dad puts on his '90s Brit-pop mix, and Millie and I look at each other and moan loudly when he and Mom start singing along together about something called a champagne supernova.

The fish tank at the front of the restaurant is filled with lucky golden yellow and bright orange koi carp. They don't seem very lucky to me, circling the tank over and over again. Or maybe the luck is for the restaurant owner, in which case it's working, because it's always full when we come in here. I look at my reflection in the tank and fiddle with the pockets of my navy blue T-shirt dress. Mom told me to change out of my T-shirt and shorts, which is my daily uniform, and this is technically a dress, although I did catch her side-eye my Birkenstocks. That was nothing compared to the side-eye she gave to Millie's spaghetti-strapped sundress. I heard her ask Ah-ma if she could let the hem down a couple of inches.

As we wait, an older couple from the local Taiwanese association walks in. Ah-ma greets them, and they make small talk in Chinese before the adults turn their eyes to me and Millie and tell Mom and Dad in English how much we've grown and how we are so beautiful (Millie) and sporty (me). Mom replies something about how we are just average and not as intelligent as their granddaughters, who are now both at Queen's University, and comments on how proud they must be. It used to bother me when she would say things like that, but I've seen it enough to understand that this verbal dance is cultural. No one ever just says *Thank you*. It's as if a compliment is some sort of booby prize, and no one wants to be left holding it.

The waiter leads us to a round table and hands each adult a menu, but Mom is the only one looking through it since she's the one that always does the ordering. I like how she always takes charge. After a few minutes of discussion with Dad and Ah-ma, Mom waves the waiter back over.

"Don't forget the spring rolls," Millie says, her eyes on her phone.

"Already ordered." She smiles. "And, girls, you're in for a treat. I prebooked a Peking duck for tonight." Mom pours fragrant jasmine tea into five cups and pushes the lazy Susan first to Ah-ma, then to Dad, then to me and Millie, taking the last one for herself.

My interest is piqued: we only get Peking duck on super-special occasions. I completely forgot she had news. She must be about to drop something big. Maybe we'll finally get to go on a trip to Disney World.

"How was the hockey game today?" Dad asks. He calls it *hockey* instead of *field hockey*, and it always confuses people when he tells them he used to play hockey on grass back at school.

"It was yesterday. We tied."

"Oh, right. And your cooking class, Millie?" Dad asks about her summer culinary camp. Millie wants to be a chef. Or a makeup artist. She changes her mind daily—sometimes even twice a day.

"Fine." Millie doesn't look up from her phone. I had to

wait until my twelfth birthday to get a phone, and Millie had such a fit that Mom and Dad got her one, too, just to keep her quiet. I said it wasn't fair and that Millie should wait a year until she turns twelve. I even heard Ah-ma complain to Mom about Millie getting spoiled, but Mom just said it was easier for everyone if they just got her a phone.

"Mom, Ah-ma said you have news?" I ask, sitting straight and attentive.

Millie doesn't look up from her phone, busy scrolling and liking random photos. I grab the phone out of her hand and put it facedown on the table.

"What the—?" She huffs, but my hard stare shuts her up.

Dad looks like he's about to burst with excitement as Mom starts to speak.

"That's right, I have something important to announce." Her voice trails off as the waiter arrives to present a whole duck, head and all, dark and shiny. Mom nods her head in approval, and the waiter slices it beside our table. Another waiter brings us woven bamboo baskets of pancakes and little dishes of spring onion, cucumber, and sweet bean sauce. We momentarily forget about Mom's news as we each grab a pancake, slather it with sauce, and stuff it with slices of juicy duck, then roll it, like a Chinese fajita. We gobble them down in three bites. As we each fill our second pancakes, Dad clears his throat and looks over at Mom. I notice she hasn't eaten her first one yet.

"Gracie," he says gently. He puts his hand over Mom's.

She nods and starts to speak. "Like I was trying to say, I have something important to announce. Something that affects the whole family."

"You girls are in for a great surprise." Dad gives us a wide grin.

"I've been offered a promotion. You're looking at the new chief operating officer for Asia-Pacific for Lo Holdings International." Her smile is huge.

Dad gazes at Mom, his eyelashes fluttering. She bites her lower lip, and her eyes flit expectantly between me and Millie.

"That's great, Mom. Congratulations." It sounds like a fancy title, even though I don't really know what it means.

"Brilliant, Mom," Millie says.

I'm about to bite into my pancake when my mom starts speaking again.

"Obviously, the COO for the Asia-Pacific role won't be based in Toronto, so in two weeks we'll be moving to Hong Kong."

2

A brief glance passes between Millie and me. She looks as confused as I am feeling.

"Did you just say we're moving to Hong Kong?" I lean forward, confident that I must have misheard, and wait for them to clarify.

"Yes," my mother and father say in unison, their hands touching.

Millie and I start talking at the same time. Or yelling, in Millie's case.

"Two weeks? This isn't fair! You're taking me away from all my friends!" Millie bangs her fist on the table.

"Hong Kong? Like the one in China?" I secretly hope

there's a Hong Kong nearby that I haven't heard of, like the London in Ontario or the Paris in Texas.

"There's *no way* I'm moving to China. They don't even have Snapchat or Instagram there." Millie slumps deeper into her chair and starts scrolling on her phone, her way of tuning out the world.

I notice the other diners look over at us curiously.

"And how long would we be going for?" My voice is a pitch higher than normal.

"The contract agreement is for two years," Mom says.

"Agreement? There's no agreement here. No one asked me!" I say, my arms folded in front of my chest. My heart is beating so fast, the blood rushing to my face makes it feel like it's on fire. "And we barely speak Chinese." The memory of being dragged kicking and screaming to years of Saturday Chinese school pops in my head.

"English is an official language in Hong Kong, so you'll have no problems getting by. And your schooling will be in English," Dad says.

"What kind of school will that be?" I don't pause to let them answer as question after question drop from my lips like a waterfall. "Do they even have school sports teams there?" I can't imagine not being part of a school team.

"Will the kids even speak English?" How will I make any friends if I can't even talk to them? "Or will I have to learn Cantonese, too?" Ah-ma told me the reason she doesn't speak Chinese with our neighbors, the Chans, is because they are from Hong Kong and speak a different form of Chinese.

"Hellooo? What about me?" Millie puts her phone down. "I'm so not going anywhere. I'll live with Violet while you're gone. I'm sure her parents won't mind. In fact, I'm sure they'll feel totally sorry for me."

"Millie, you will do no such thing. Your mother and I would never leave you behind to live with your friend. Besides, you're only eleven." He tries to touch her hand, but she pulls it away and pouts. She's only a year and three months younger than me, but the baby of the family.

"We are *all* going, end of story," Mom says, gently but firmly.

Millie balls her fists and pushes her chair back and stands up so quickly that the waiter doesn't have time to react and move around her. The tray loaded with spring rolls, sweet plum sauce, and steamed spinach goes flying in the air. I watch, frozen in my seat as the various bits of food crash-land on the floor beside us, narrowly missing

28

the people at the next table. The restaurant goes quiet. Even the random bored little kids running between tables have stopped to stare, their eyes as wide as steamed pork buns.

"Amelia-Tian Jones, sit down this instant," Dad says in a sharp and stern tone. He must be super angry if he's calling Millie by her full name.

Mom's eyes start to well up. I've hardly ever seen my mom upset, and I feel a pang of guilt. I know this must be a big deal for her, but I can't help but think this isn't fair—they didn't even discuss this with us before deciding. Dad is obviously too annoyed to talk and simply glares at Millie until she slinks back in her chair, shamefacedly looking at the two waiters quietly cleaning up the mess on the floor.

It's Ah-ma who steps in and breaks the silence. "Your mama work so hard. She do what is expected of her, and now is successful and have good career. Good career to make life good for you, but you both sound so ungrateful."

She wags her finger at me and Millie. I feel my cheeks burn, and I look down at my hands, not daring to glance at my mother.

I know my mom works hard, and whenever we complain about her being at the office late or away on another business trip, Dad reminds us that her job is what helps pay for the nice things we have, like summer cottage rentals in Muskoka or winter skiing in Quebec. And now my mom is Gracie Li-Jones, chief of something at a big international company, so I should be happy for her, happy for us. But instead, all I feel is a big knot in the pit of my stomach thinking about how we are going to be taken away from everything and everyone we know. And in two weeks!

"Well, Dad, what about your job?" I ask.

Dad casts a quick glance at Mom and clears his throat. Dad is a professor. Professor Jones, "Like in *Indiana Jones*," he likes to joke, much to our embarrassment. His specialty is Sino-British history, which is basically stuff that happened a long time ago, like the British colonization of Hong Kong and its handover back to China.

"I've been granted a leave of absence from the university, and I'm excited to start writing that long-planned-for novel. And it'll be nice to live in the same city as my brother and his family." He's referring to Uncle Charlie, his wife, and my twin cousins, who moved from London to Hong Kong ages ago. I guess moving to Hong Kong won't be that bad if we have family there. I haven't seen those cousins for years. I can't even remember what they look like, other than that they are blond. It's not like Mom's side of the family. She has a gazillion cousins who live in Canada and the US, and all the families meet up for a reunion every year. It's so much fun: all the kids play board games and charades, and of course, complain about our parents.

"What about you, Ah-ma? Are you happy about moving to Hong Kong?" I look over at my grandmother.

"I will be staying here, baobei." Ah-ma gives me a faint smile and a pat on the shoulder.

I bolt up in my seat. "What do you mean? You aren't coming?" My voice squeaks as a lump forms and gets stuck in my throat.

"Your move only temporary," says Ah-ma. "I have my friends and my church, and Uncle Eli and his family nearby." Mom's younger brother lives in some suburb up north. "They have new baby and need me."

I want to yell that we need her, too, that we need her more, but I know that wouldn't be fair of me to say. Ah-ma reaches under the table and squeezes my hand. I let it rest in hers, soothed by its warmth.

Mom and Dad give us more detail about the move and try and talk it up. *What a great opportunity your mom has been offered. School places and tuition in a top private school. A huge apartment on the beach and hiking in our backyard. You can get to know your cousins better. Plenty of outdoor pursuits.*

I keep quiet. I'm about to leave my whole life behind. I've been going to Maple Grove since kindergarten, and I don't want to leave my friends, even if friendships are a little bumpy right now. But mostly, I can't imagine the idea of a new home in Hong Kong without the smell of Ah-ma's Chinese ointments, the sight of pink curlers in her hair at breakfast, or the sound of her laughing along with her favorite Taiwanese game shows. And what about our ritual Friday evenings, where we all crowd on the sofa to watch a movie and pass a giant bowl of fresh popcorn sprinkled with sugar and salt? Or Sunday mornings, when Dad makes his famous fluffy pancakes? And with Mom's fancy new job, is she still going to be able to tuck me in and kiss me good-night? It seems like in two weeks, it's not just our location that will change but that everything about my life is going to change, too.

3

The next morning, there's a gentle knock at my bedroom door, and Ah-ma comes in, her slippers shuffling on the floor. She sits on the edge of my bed.

"Baobei, you have slept in."

I rub my eyes and turn to check the clock on my phone: it's almost nine. I never wake up this late, since we normally have stuff to do, like go to the farmers market or pop into the local library. From the window, the sky looks sunny and bright, the opposite of my mood.

"Is everyone home?"

"No, your mama and baba have gone for a walk. But Amelia-Tian is in her room. Her door is locked. She still very upset."

"I'm upset, too." I sit up and fold my arms across my chest. "Aren't you sad that we're leaving?" *Sad that you won't be with us?* I want to ask. "Did they even ask you before they decided?"

My nose starts running as I think about living without Ah-ma. She passes me a tissue from her pocket.

"Don't worry about me. I told you, I have lots of friends and your uncle Eli close by. And the weather in Hong Kong is too hot for me. More hotter than Taiwan." She starts smoothing out the edges of my blue-striped cotton duvet cover. "Besides, you are only going for two years."

"Two years—that's forever!" I know I'm exaggerating, but it feels like we're going for an eternity.

Ah-ma pats my leg, her jade bangle that she always wears knocks and tickles my kneecap. "You know, your mama work very hard. When we moved here from Taiwan, I made her study, she study so hard. No time for friends, no time for play, only time for study. She follow rules, like good immigrant. At work, she swallowed a lot of bitterness to reach top position. She need to prove herself more because she is woman and mother. Now she is big boss, and moving to Hong Kong will let her be even bigger boss. It is reward for all the bitterness."

I try not to roll my eyes. I've heard the chi ku—*swallow bitterness*—speech many times. Why do Ah-ma and all the aunties and uncles talk about the need to suffer before being happy? Like, since they already went through it, wouldn't they want to make sure we don't have to? I ball up my tissue and throw it at the garbage can, which I miss completely.

Ah-ma smiles and touches my hand. I throw my arms around her and bury my head in her neck, inhaling the perfumed scent of her face cream.

Mom pokes her head in my room. "We're back from our walk. Are you up for going to the farmers market? I'll let you pick a treat."

I don't answer, but look at Ah-ma. I want to stay in this comfortable spot with her on my bed. As if she can read my mind, she says, "Go, and when you come back, we'll make lunch together. Jiaozi." Dumplings, my favorite.

"Hao ba." *Fine.*

I quickly change out of my pajamas into my Raptors T-shirt and denim shorts. As I brush my teeth, I look in the mirror. Will there be many people in Hong Kong that are mixed-race like me? Here in Toronto, it's not exactly that I feel like I don't fit in, but more like I stand out, like when

35

people say I look *exotic* or ask me where I'm *really* from, and by that they don't mean Canada. Even in our extended family, Millie and I are the only two who are mixed, so I've heard some aunties comment on my tan from playing sports. Once a cousin in Taiwan asked why my nose was so big. It's a normal-looking nose, but I have a bridge like most white people. Mom says it's *European*. No one ever says anything about Millie. Except for her wavy hair, she is more classically half-Chinese-looking, with light skin and a little button nose. Once we move to Hong Kong, I wonder if I'll see more people that look like me. I guess only time will tell.

Millie ignored all of the pleas to open her door. She's always the one stomping her feet and throwing tantrums to get her way, so I'm not surprised. And this time it's more than a little understandable. It's just Mom, Dad, and me biking over to the market. Armed with our cloth shopping bags, we go from stall to stall loading up on fresh local fruit and vegetables. At a stall piled high with jars of golden honey, on display is an article cut out from a magazine mentioning all the famous people who have bought the honey.

"It's the who's who of Toronto high society," the man running the stall says.

Mom smiles politely and leads us away, muttering, "High society? That's so ridiculous."

While Dad is busy smelling mushrooms, I check out the next aisle, and my heart skips a beat. It's Natalie. Do I go talk to her and tell her my news? It's huge news, and I want to share it with her. But after yesterday in the cafeteria, I'm not sure how she'll react. Will she even miss me?

"Mom, can I go get the cherries now?"

"Sure. I don't see why not." Mom reaches for her wallet. "Here's ten dollars. Meet us right back here when you're done."

"Yup," I say, already running toward where I spotted Natalie, hoping that she's going to throw her arms around me when she finds out about Hong Kong and that we'll completely forget about these last few weeks.

"Holly-Mei!" she says, her face lighting up.

My heart jumps when I see her smile. "I have some news. Can we talk over there?" I point to some picnic tables by the organic lemonade stand.

Her smile fades. "Um, now?"

I follow her eyes and see two girls with matching sparkly backpacks. I know who those belong to. "Are you here with Katie and Ellie?"

As if on cue, the two girls come over.

"Natalie, last night was so fun, wasn't it?" Katie asks with a smirk.

"I hardly got any sleep," Ellie says.

My eyes open wide. "Did you have a sleepover without me?" I ask, incredulous.

Natalie looks momentarily frozen before she gives me a meek nod. I can't breathe for a second; it feels like there's a weight on my chest. Our regular sleepovers are sacred. And just because we haven't had one this month, I never expected her to have one without me. To *replace* me.

My cheeks flush, and I feel sick. I quickly turn my back and head toward my parents.

"Wait, don't go. What's your news?" I hear Natalie ask, her voice fading as I pick up my pace.

I find Mom and Dad and tell them I'm going home because my stomach aches. Dad says we'll all go together, but I tell them to keep shopping. "Don't forget the cherries," I say, handing back Mom's money. They look a little puzzled but just shrug and tell me to text when I arrive home safely.

As I pedal home, all I can think is: Who needs these jerks? Maybe this move won't be so bad after all. What do I have to lose? I've already lost all my friends, including my supposed best friend, and being friendless in my final year at Maple Grove Elementary would definitely be a nightmare. The more I think about it, the more this move to the opposite end of the world sounds like the answer to all my problems. I can start fresh, and everything will be perfect.

With that thought firmly in my head, I skip into the house and join Ah-ma in the kitchen. She looks at me quizzically. "Where are your parents?"

"Still shopping." I text Mom to tell her I'm home.

She shrugs and nods at the sink, a hint for me to wash my hands, while she starts getting the ingredients for the dumpling dough ready.

Ah-ma measures the flour and puts a few cups in a large stainless-steel mixing bowl. I slowly pour some water in as she stirs the mixture vigorously with a pair of wooden chopsticks.

"Here, you knead. I start chopping," she says as she hands me the bowl.

We're having vegetable dumplings. Millie is on a kick about us eating less meat, and she's downloaded all these new recipes for us to try. I start pounding and squeezing the dough. The mushy mess flowing between my fingers is relaxing.

"I visit Hong Kong once, in the 1960s. Interesting city with lots of history. You will fit in and make new friends after a few weeks." Ah-ma stops chopping the shiitake mushrooms and looks up for a response as if she had just asked me a question.

"A few weeks? I'm sure I'll make new friends right away." *Better friends than the ones here, no question.* "And I'm sure fitting in will be a piece of cake." I pick at the gooey dough from my hands and push them back into the ball, like I'm pushing away any worries I had earlier about standing out.

Ah-ma looks at me and raises an eyebrow. I know that look. Mom can do the one-raised-eyebrow thing, too. It means she doesn't believe me. But I believe me.

"What? I'll play team sports, and I'll make instant friends."

Ah-ma throws the mushrooms into a big bowl and moves onto chopping the block of tofu and leafy bok choy. "You are adaptable, like me. But moving to a new country take time to adjust. I just want you being realistic."

"I am being realistic." This plan is perfect. New country, new school, new friends.

Ah-ma lets out a big sigh. "You know, I followed husband to new country with two children. I was graduate

41

of art history from Taida, the Harvard of Taiwan. But with no English, I cannot get job. So I stay home and raise family." Ah-ma grabs the chives and garlic and quickly but forcefully chops them, making little *bang, bang, bang* noises on the wooden cutting board. I stare at her fingers, counting them, making sure she hasn't lost any. She puts all the ingredients in a bowl, sets down her knife, and looks at me. "It was lonely at beginning. But we made lot of friends who also move from Taiwan. They became our family. Your Ah-gong get good job at the university here—microbiology professor with tenure. And even though I not working, I used my time to become better painter."

"Your paintings are beautiful, Ah-ma." My eyes turn to the painting in the living room above the sofa, visible from the open kitchen. The pink lotus is so lifelike, I always forget it's not a photograph. "So you ended up happy you moved?"

"There is a saying: ku jin gan lai—*bitterness finishes, sweetness begins*. The move may be hard at first, but you will eventually find happiness," Ah-ma says.

"Why do I need to go through bitterness first?" I've had my bitterness already. "Hong Kong is going to be pure sweetness."

I reach for the dough to start rolling and filling it. But Ah-ma takes the bowl from me and covers it with a tea towel.

"We need to let dough sit for one hour before filling," Ah-ma says. "Patience, baobei."

By two o'clock, Millie hasn't come out of her room, so I load up a tray with a plate of dumplings and a bowl of the cherries my parents brought back from the market.

"I come bearing gifts," I say as I knock on her door.

She opens the door a crack, looks down at the steaming dumplings, and lets me in. She must have slept in the dress she wore last night. I place the plate and dipping sauce on her desk in the only spot not covered with papers, colored markers, and books.

She takes a bite. "Good, but the dipping sauce would be better with a bit of shredded ginger," she says. "I saw it on YouTube."

Millie is always sharing random cooking ideas with us. She likes putting her own spin on food. I just follow recipes or Ah-ma's instructions and never deviate. Ah-ma says recipes are like rules: best to follow them.

"You will be happy to hear that there's YouTube in Hong Kong. And Insta and Snapchat," I say.

She wolfs down the dumplings and asks me to get her a glass of water from the kitchen so she can avoid bumping into anyone. When I get back to her room, she thanks me and offers me a red Twizzler, my favorite treat, from the secret candy stash in her desk, then she flops back on her bed. I sit down and lean against her headboard and loop a curl of her long hair around my finger as I nibble on my licorice stick.

"Millie, I know you think this move sucks. But maybe there are some good things about it."

"What are we even going to do there?"

"It's going to be amazing. We'll have an apartment on the beach. The beach, Millie! The ocean! Hong Kong is subtropical like Taiwan, so I bet we can hang outside all year round."

"No snow?" She looks over at me, eyes wide. I'm also excited at the prospect of a winter without five months of snow.

"Nope. And I bet you can try surfing." She loves watching old episodes of *Bondi Rescue* because of all the cute surfers.

Millie bolts up in bed. "Really, you think?"

"For sure." I laugh at how easy it is to cheer her up.

"Let's look up this new school. I bet it'll be amazing, and we'll make tons of new friends."

"I'm not the one that needs new friends," she says.

I let go of her hair and slump back against the headboard.

"Sorry," she says. "Low blow."

"It's fine. I'm completely over it." This move is going to fix everything.

She jumps out of bed and grabs a box of Pocky sticks from her stash and waves them under my nose, like some sort of peace offering. "Green matcha, my new discovery."

I take one with a smile. "I bet we'll find some awesome new snacks in Hong Kong."

We tiptoe past Mom and Dad's shared home office toward the living room like we're on a spy mission. I log into the kids' computer, which is Mom's old work laptop perched on an antique desk in the corner, since Millie's phone has been confiscated by Dad and mine is charging. I type in the name of the school, Tai Tam Prep, and we look through the images together.

"The school is on the waterfront and has its own beach." I'm impressed. It's what I'd imagine Hawaii would look like.

"Type in *surf beach Hong Kong*," Millie says, apparently not interested in researching any more about the school itself. When the images open, her *ooh*s and *aah*s fill my ears.

"Move over," she says, pushing her way onto the single chair at the desk. I get up and let her have it. She pulls up Google Maps. "Look, Hong Kong is not that far from Korea." She starts to get all starry-eyed. "Maybe we can go on holiday there."

"And chase down BTS and Blackpink?" I say, laughing.

"Dare to dream, Holly-Mei." Millie giggles.

"I'd go to Seoul just for the snacks." I smack my lips thinking of the kimbap rice rolls Millie made last month.

As we soak up image after image of Hong Kong, I get butterflies of excitement in my stomach. Yes, the fancy school, beach, and all my soon-to-be new friends sound amazing, but so does living in a whole new country. I'm going to try to convince my parents to take us for a holiday to hike the Great Wall of China or see the pandas in Chengdu.

I look up and see Ah-ma watching us from the hallway as she sips tea from her favorite mug. She smiles and nods at me. As she shuffles away, the scent of her Tiger Balm lingers in the air, just like all my hopes and excitement for this fresh new start.

4

My jaw drops when I see the huge seats for our fifteen-hour flight to Hong Kong. I've been on a plane before, but have always sat tightly packed at the back, never in business class.

"Are these really our seats?" I ask Mom, impressed. I nestle under a down-filled duvet and tuck a matching silk pillowcase under my head. I rip open the complimentary toiletry bag waiting for me on my tabletop.

"Do we get to keep all this free stuff?" I pull the items out one by one: toothbrush; mouthwash; satin sleep-mask; earplugs; and porcelain pots of scented cream.

Millie is already dabbing the fragrant French cream

all over her face when the flight attendant comes by and offers us mango smoothies and truffle chocolates.

"I could get used to this." Millie sighs as she pops a second piece of chocolate into her mouth and licks the cocoa powder off her fingers.

"Don't get too comfortable!" I laugh, but I wouldn't mind getting used to it. I take a sip of my smoothie and wonder if Mom's promotion means we get to fly more often, and with treats like this.

Millie has slowly come around to the move over the past two weeks. When we were doing research on the living-room computer, we found some drone footage of Hong Kong on YouTube that showcased the size of the city: it's bigger than any city either of us has ever been to, but still full of little markets and alleys that look fun to explore. Mom told us that we wouldn't need to share a computer anymore; all Tai Tam Prep students get their own, meaning we *each* get a brand-new MacBook Air for school. Dad joked that his daughters would have newer tech than he has. Then Mom dropped the bombshell that Grade 7 at this new school is actually the first year of *Upper School*, meaning I'm going to be one of the babies of the school, while Millie and her classmates get to rule over the *Lower*

School. After hearing that, Millie slowly reduced her whining about leaving school and all her friends.

I've been full on excited about this move after the initial shock. Not only about the new friends I'm going to make and fun stuff I'm going to do, but also about getting to experience my heritage firsthand. Especially the food! They say that you can learn a lot about a culture through its food, and I fully intend to try all the snacks I can get my hands on. I've even made a list of things to try, like dan tat, egg waffles, and pineapple buns. I've had them in Toronto, but I can't wait to try the original Hong Kong versions. I only wish Ah-ma would have moved with us. She's going to be the part of home I'll miss the most. But she did promise to video-call me on her iPad for weekly catch-ups after I showed her how easy it was. Hopefully I'll also be able to show her how easy it is to fall into my fabulous new life in Hong Kong.

I see Millie returning from the galley with her arm full of snacks, and I pause my movie.

"Look at all this free stuff! Want some chips? I've got Godiva chocolates and a pear, too," she says.

"They're going to serve dinner in a minute." I reach

for a bag of chips anyway. I can't ever say no to salt and vinegar flavor.

"What are you watching?" she asks.

"*Clueless*. I haven't seen it in ages."

"What are you? Stuck in the '90s?"

"Look, it's Kristy's mom from *The Baby-Sitters Club*." I point to the screen. "What about you?"

"An *Avengers* marathon, you know, because Thor." Millie plops back into her seat.

I rip open the chips, put my Bose headphones back on, and rewind to the beginning of the film. Cher is going through her closet choices on her computer to find the best outfit for the first day of school. Mom said we'd have a uniform at our new school, so thankfully I won't need to start worrying about what I wear. I hope it'll be as comfortable as my current uniform of T-shirt, leggings, and hoodie.

After the movie ends, I flick through a Hong Kong fashion magazine the flight attendant hands out. All of the feminine and delicate models look like Snow White: skin white as snow, lips red as blood, and long hair black as ebony. I instinctively touch my straight ponytail, another part of my uniform, and wonder if my hair would be as bouncy as the hair in the ads if I left it down. They all have dainty manicured hands, too. I look down at my short unpainted nails and smother on the fancy French hand cream from my toiletry bag.

I pick up another magazine hoping for something interesting on Hong Kong pop culture or tourist sites, but it's the same as the last one, and I throw it down in frustration.

"Honey, what's up?" My mom is grabbing something from the overhead bin.

"Oh, nothing. These magazines are so boring—they're just full of ads." I pick one up and point to all the images of jewelry and high-end fashion. "What if the kids in Hong Kong are like Cher with her giant rotating closet?"

Mom laughs and kneels down at my seat. "What are you talking about?"

"Or what about these models with their creams that promise to whiten and brighten my skin? What does that even mean?" I look over at Millie, whose face looks more like the girls in the ads than mine does.

"Those ads are peddling nonsense. Some people mistakenly believe that lighter is better, more beautiful. But your olive complexion is absolutely beautiful just the

51

color it is." Mom touches my cheek and strokes it with her thumb. She always has a way of knowing the right thing to say. "Look, I need to read through some documents. We'll chat later, okay?"

I pass her the pile of magazines and start browsing the movies.

I wake up from a fitful nap and head through the darkened cabin toward the galley to get a midnight snack. I hear a *tap tap tap* noise. I look around, thinking it might be the little teacup poodle I saw earlier. The sound gets louder the closer I get to the front, but no one else seems to hear with their headphones on or earplugs in, and the crew is behind the curtain. Then I hear it. A little, muffled "Help?" coming from the bathroom.

"Hello?" I say, gently knocking on the door. "Are you okay?"

"The door is stuck. I can't open the lock."

"Press the button to call the attendant."

"I've tried that already!" The voice sounds exasperated.

I pull the latch, but it's locked from the inside. I rattle it, but it doesn't budge. I have an idea. I grab a coin from my hoodie pocket, and it fits perfectly into the groove of the lock. "Hold on," I say as I turn the lock, but the person inside pushes the door at the same time and comes tumbling out, landing on me. A girl straightens herself out and pushes back her shiny, bouncy, black hair.

"Thanks." She smiles with obvious relief. "I was stuck there for, like, half an hour." She looks as feminine and delicate as the models in the magazine. "I'm so thirsty," she says as she heads behind the curtain to the galley. I follow her. She tells the flight attendant about the lock and orders a sparkling water and a wonton noodle soup.

"That sounds yummy. I'm going to copy you," I say.

"I get this all the time. Although their dan dan mian in the lounge at the Hong Kong airport is the best. It's so peanuty."

"Peanut butter makes everything taste good," I say, smacking my lips.

"Aren't lounges the best?"

"Duh, yeah, of course." I'm happy the cabin lights are dimmed so she doesn't see the flash of red in my cheeks. How many lounges has this girl been in?

"I can't wait to get back to get back to Hong Kong. I miss my puppy, Cookie."

"Cute name. So you live in Hong Kong? We're moving there."

"Really? You'll love it. It's so amazing," she says, gushing.

"What were you doing in Toronto?" I ask.

Her eyes dart around, and her smile fades. What did I say? Why is she being weird all of a sudden?

A little *ping* goes off behind me, and the flight attendant appears with a tray on which rest a large steaming bowl, a porcelain spoon, and set of silver chopsticks. "Shall I take these to your seat?"

"No, thank you." The girl turns to me as she takes the tray. "See you. Enjoy the wontons."

As I wait for my food, I can't help but think how cool and friendly she was. I'm sure I was just imagining her weird reaction. When we land, I'm going to get her name and number so we can hang out. If everyone in Hong Kong is like her, then I'm completely right about how easy it's going to be to meet people and make friends at my new school. I'm going to tell Ah-ma to update her old-fashioned bitterness saying, because life in Hong Kong is going to be nothing but sweet.

I walk back to my seat with my wontons, and my mom looks up at me and pats her footrest. She moves her laptop and papers away so I can sit down, and we squeeze together.

"I know this isn't easy for you and your sister. But I promise you, it'll be such a great life experience." She reaches over and touches my knee. "You know, this school will be more academic and competitive than Maple Grove."

"I'm a good student," I say.

"You'll need to study hard. Harder." She bites her lip before saying, "You might need to reconsider all the sports activities you do."

I want to argue and ask where this sudden terrible idea has come from, but hold my tongue because I have a tray of piping hot soup balancing on my lap.

"You'll have so many new opportunities, so many things to see and do in Asia," she says.

"I'm pretty excited."

"And of course, it's normal to be nervous and scared, too," she says.

I see the fashion magazines by her feet, and I push thoughts about those ads to the back of my head. "I'm not scared at all." I shake my head for emphasis.

Mom puts her arm around my shoulder and gives

me a little hug. "And the people you'll meet are in a dif-ferent sphere."

My head pops off her shoulder. "Different sphere?"

"The kids at school won't just be the children of doc-tors, lawyers, and academics. They will be the heirs to mul-tinational, billion-dollar companies. You'll meet all the right people in Hong Kong. The best of society." Mom beams.

Mom's never talked about the *right people* or *society* before. What does the *right people* even mean? And why does my mother suddenly care about this?

5

We walk out of baggage claim into the modern arrivals terminal. Millie giggles at the name of the airport, Chek Lap Kok, and all three of us raise our eyebrows. She apologizes and says she's just tired. But still, she can't wipe the smirk from her face. I look around for the girl from the bathroom, but don't see her anywhere.

Waiting for us outside in the arrivals lounge is a man with a sign that says *Li-Jones Family*. Dad points at the sign, looks at me and Millie, and shrugs like he's thinking *I'd better get used to our new name—Mom's the big boss here*. Mom touches his shoulder and reassures him that we are still the Jones family and she's the only Li-Jones. Then she is business as usual, directing the man in

Mandonese—a hybrid of Mandarin and Cantonese, of which I only understand a fragment. I think it's pretty cool that she takes charge and people listen. The man takes us and our bag-laden trolleys down the hall to the VIP lounge area.

Millie looks like she's about to burst. "VIP! Ma, are you a VIP now?"

"Don't get overexcited. I'm just a small player in the company," my mom says modestly, but we all know why we're in Hong Kong. She's now a top player for one of those *multinational, billion-dollar companies* she mentioned earlier. I look over at her and smile proudly even though her comment about the *right people* is still swirling in my head.

A black van pulls up to the door of the lounge, and we step outside. It's so humid and hot, the air feels like a heavy blanket, and beads of sweat start dripping down my face.

"What's that Finnish word for the steam that rises after you throw water on the rocks in a sauna? That's how hot and muggy it feels here," my dad says, reading my mind.

"Löyly, right?" I say.

"Why do you even know that?" Millie asks.

"Because she listens. Remember when I told you about that conference I went to in Helsinki?" my dad asks.

"Nope," Millie says.

"Precisely," he says.

The van is packed with the eight large suitcases we brought with us on the plane—everything we need for the next two years. Mom told us that our apartment, or *flat* as they say in this former British colony, is company-owned and comes fully furnished. She also told us to pack a maximum of two suitcases as we'll have school uniforms and won't need as many clothes. Plus she offered to buy us new things once we got to Hong Kong, in case we forgot anything. I would love a pair of Lululemon running leggings, but somehow I doubt Mom meant new sportswear.

Out the window, green hills rise on one side and the sea opens on the other. As we drive toward Kowloon over a suspended bridge, we pass what looks like a minicity of giant colored Lego blocks and rows and rows of massive cranes.

"What is that place? It looks like something off a sci-fi film set," I say, imagining the giant blocks coming to life and trampling the city.

"That's our company's shipping port. Those containers are filled with stuff made in China. They get loaded onto cargo ships and sent around the world," Mom says.

"So that's the Lo Holdings sign on all the cranes?" Dad asks.

"Yes." Mom smiles with pride.

"So impressive." Dad whistles. "What about the ships?"

"Most belong to Fitzwilliam Shipping," Mom says.

"Not a Chinese company?" Dad asks.

"They're actually based in Hong Kong. Both the Lo and Fitzwilliam families have been around since the late 1800s."

It must be interesting to have such deep roots in a place. Most people I know, their parents, grandparents, or great-grandparents moved to Canada from somewhere else.

"Oh, yes," Dad says. "Rumor has it that many of the British merchants of that era made their money during the Opium Wars, and some were even pirates."

Whoa, pirates! I need to look up more about Hong Kong history when I get my laptop.

When we emerge from the tunnel under the harbor, Mom says excitedly, "This is Hong Kong Island."

I look over the water. It's busy with dozens of boats of different sizes—ferries, tugboats, and cruise ships. Tall buildings, some that seem to touch the sky, line both sides of the harbor.

After a minute Mom says, "This is Central, the main business area." She waves to the left. "And there is my office." She points to the tallest building in the skyline—a sleek modern glass building. It has the logo of her company on the side, the same one as on all the cranes back at the shipping port. A simple overlapped red *L* and *H* inside a white circle.

"Does the whole building belong to your firm?" Dad asks.

"The whole city block belongs to us." Her eyes twinkle.

I have to stretch my neck to see the tops of all these high-rises, and it feels like I've traveled to some future universe. Everything around me is gleaming glass and steel like nothing I've ever seen before, even more futuristic than Toronto or Taipei, or pictures I've seen of New York or Tokyo. I don't know if my head is spinning because of jet lag or because of my new surroundings.

We pass through another tunnel, this time through a leafy hill. When we get to the other side, Mom announces that we're on the South Side. The big-city feel is gone, replaced by lots of trees, some low-rise buildings, and a road that winds along the sea. The sun is already down past the horizon, and the sky is orange and pink.

"We're almost home," she says.

Home.

It's getting dark by the time we pull into the circular driveway of our building complex, Lofty Heights. A row of imposing towers faces the sea. There are only two apartments on our floor. When we open the front door and walk inside, it feels like endless space. Floor-to-ceiling windows lead to a balcony overlooking the water. Everything is modern and luxurious, light and bright, even though it's nighttime. Mom says it's *Nordic chic*, but that makes me think of log cabins surrounded by trees, so I'm not really sure what she means.

"Discuss and decide which room you're each taking," Mom says to me and Millie.

"Dibs on this one." Millie throws her backpack onto the bed in the room with the sea view.

It's typical Millie to take what she wants first before thinking. "Whatever, I don't care." I shrug and walk into the room across from hers. "This one is bigger anyway."

"Really?" she asks in a whiny voice as she tries to peer into my room, but I close the door on her.

In my carry-on I find one of Ah-ma's silk scarves that I took as a souvenir and breathe in her scent—a mix of camphor, menthol, and lavender. I don't bother opening my suitcase to find my pajamas. I just brush my teeth and jump into bed in my underwear.

I'm woken up by the sun shining through the open blinds. The view from my room faces the rolling green hills, and I'm pretty pleased with it. I stumble out of bed and into my en suite bathroom, which is bigger than my entire bedroom back in Toronto. I can't believe I don't need to share a bathroom with Millie anymore. So many times I've almost been late for school because Millie was busy fussing with her hair. The rain shower is like a warm waterfall massaging my head. I throw on the first T-shirt and shorts I find in my suitcase and head out to explore the flat. The other bedroom doors are closed, so I tiptoe into the living room in case everyone is still sleeping. I can't believe the view: the sea is sparkling in the sunshine like it's decorated with fairy lights. In the distance I see some little islands, and at the foot of our building is a crescent-shaped beach where I can make out pontoons and some swimmers. I can't wait to try swimming in the sea. Natalie and those girls can have Lake Ontario. I've got the South China Sea in my front yard.

The smell of frying bacon reaches my nose, and I follow it toward the kitchen, thinking Dad must be up after all. My stomach rumbles and I enter, expecting to find my father flipping pancakes, but instead there is an Asian lady in front of the stove being directed by my mom. I look from her to the lady and back to my mom, waiting for someone to fill me in on what's going on. The lady is shorter but looks a touch older than my mom. Her thick black hair is tied back, and she's wearing a flowery top and indoor slippers, like the kind Ah-ma wears.

"Hi," I say to both of them.

"Good morning!" Mom says, giving me a peck on

the cheek. "Did you sleep well? Your father and sister are still asleep."

"I think I slept for, like, fifteen hours." I stretch my arms above my head and move my neck side to side to get the kinks out.

"This is Joy." Mom introduces me to the lady pouring batter into the frying pan. "She's going to help us with household duties."

"Hi, I'm Holly-Mei."

"Nice to meet you. Would you like some pancakes and bacon?"

"Yes, please." If Mom weren't here, I'd wolf down the whole stack, I'm so hungry.

As I make my way to the dining room, I hear Joy ask if *ma'am* and *sir* would like anything else for breakfast.

My mom joins me at the table, a cup of coffee and a can of maple syrup in hand. "I picked it up at the airport. I didn't know if we could easily find it here."

I pour the amber-colored goodness onto my breakfast.

"Um, so is Joy going to cook for us every day?" I ask. These pancakes are even fluffier than Dad's.

"Yes, except Sundays, of course. We're fortunate to have her. She's from the Philippines, and her living quarters are behind the kitchen."

"She's going to live with us?" I whisper, my mouth full of pancakes.

"Yes, it's the law. She needs to live with us for her visa. She's called a helper." She spoons some sugar into her coffee.

"What about her family?"

"Her family is back home in the Philippines. People move abroad for better work opportunities."

"Kind of like us?"

"Yes, like us, I suppose." Mom nods and reaches over to pat my hand. "She'll be helping with the cooking, cleaning, and grocery shopping. And babysitting when needed."

"I'm too old for a babysitter!" I sit up straight, my fork in the air.

When Mom starts laughing, I realize she's joking. "But on a more serious note, I fully expect you and your sister to maintain your chores, just like at home. You both still have responsibilities." She dabs stray sugar crystals with her fingertip and lets them fall into her coffee.

I think about it as I chew. I feel a tiny bit strange that we have someone to look after us, but mostly I feel grateful and super lucky, especially if these super-fluffy pancakes are anything to go by.

6

I have a dream about the Dragon Gate. Yesterday when we walked down to the beach, Mom explained what the hole is that's built into one of the towers of our complex.

"It's the Dragon Gate. It allows the wind to blow from the sea to the mountains, without being blocked by the building. It's supposed to be good feng shui."

In my dream, I'm on the back of a golden dragon that flies from the leafy hills through the big square gate out toward the sea. I leap off the dragon and plunge into the cool water. That's when I wake up. I glance at my phone. Five thirty. I try to fall back asleep but am too wide-awake thinking about the first day of school. I can't believe it's today. We just got here three days ago.

I hop out of bed and go outside in my polka-dot pajamas and sit on the cushioned rattan sofa on the balcony. It's not dark anymore, but the sun is not yet up. Dad says this time of day is called twilight. I stare out at the sky, which turns from gray to orange to pink and finally to bright blue when the sun peeks its head over the hills.

My phone pings.

AH-MA: *Good luck at school today, baobei!*

ME: *Miss you!*

I take a photo of the beach and send it to her. I feel like a bad granddaughter for being a bit disappointed that it was Ah-ma writing to me and not Natalie. I was secretly hoping that she would reach out and apologize.

A light, sweet citrus scent drifts toward me. It's Mom, dressed in a crisp white blouse and a black pencil skirt with red beaded earrings dangling from her ears.

"Are you going to the office now?"

"Not yet, but I was so nervous about my first day of work that I couldn't wait to get dressed and ready. How

68

about you? How are you feeling about your first day of school?"

"Excited. This school is going to be so much better than Maple Grove."

She raises an eyebrow, just like Ah-ma does, and sits down on the sofa beside me. "Different, but not necessarily better. Are you not nervous at all?"

"No. I can't wait to dive in." And make new friends and forget about everyone back home.

"Thank you for being so brave about this move. I hope you have a great day." She reaches over and gives me a peck on the cheek. As she wipes off the traces of lipstick, she says, "Make a good impression today, okay?"

I roll my eyes as she turns to go inside. *Make a good impression*. I think back to what she said on the plane. *You'll meet all the right people in Hong Kong. The best of society.* I wonder what Dad would make of what Mom just said.

The school uniform is surprisingly simple, consisting of a white golf shirt with a navy Tai Tam Prep crest and a navy skirt. Millie is fidgeting with her collar in front of the mirror. Up, down, up, down. But she needn't be nervous.

She's going into Grade 6, the big cheese of the small kids' school.

"Do you think I can wear these shoes?" Millie slips on her leopard-print ballet flats.

"They need to be black." I tie the laces on my black low-top Converse.

"But there are black spots on the shoes," she says.

"Can't you just resist the urge to stand out for just one day?"

"Fiiine." She grabs a pair of plain black ballet flats.

The four of us head to Uncle Charlie's place in the next tower block for a quick family reunion before we jump on the school bus with the twins—Rosie and Rhys. My cousins are the same age as me, but I don't really know them that well because they've lived far away for so long. Uncle Charlie is an airline pilot. They just returned from a trip to London last night so we haven't had a chance to catch up yet.

We step into the gleaming elevator, and I scan the buttons.

"There's no fourth floor in the elevator," I say.

"They call it a *lift* here," Dad says.

"That's because the number four in Chinese, *si* or *sei*, sounds like the word for *death*," Mom says.

"I would wager that there is no Tower 4, either," Dad says.

"That's just weird," Millie says.

"Like having no thirteenth floor?" I ask.

Dad nods.

"Then, it's not so weird," I say in Millie's direction. She sticks her tongue out at me.

"I can't believe we start school today. It's only mid-August," Millie says. "I'm not ready to open books again." She seems nervous. I wonder if it's the books or the needing to make new friends that she's worried about. I give her a little squeeze, hoping some of my excitement will pass on to her.

The doorbell chimes like Big Ben, making Millie giggle. Uncle Charlie opens the door and greets Dad with a bear hug.

"Come in, come in! Welcome to Hong Kong! It's just brilliant that you guys have moved here, absolutely brilliant." He turns and yells down the hall, "Hels, they're here!"

Hels, aka Auntie Helen, comes bounding into the foyer, her blond hair bouncing, the front streak of gray

71

sparkling. "Welcome, darlings," she says. "My, have you two grown! I wouldn't have recognized you if I saw you on the high street." She pinches Millie's and my cheeks with her ruby-red manicured fingers.

Rosie runs in and gives us all a warm hug. Her blond hair is pulled into a loose bun and smells of mint shampoo, and the school skirt shows off her long ballerina legs.

"We're so pleased you're here. We're going to have so much fun!" she says.

I beam back at her. "Of course we are. I can't wait!" I'm so happy she's as excited as I am.

Rhys strolls toward us and gives Dad a handshake. He gives Mom, Millie, and me a quick hug. "Great to see you guys again!" he says as we all go into the living room. He is a couple of inches shorter than Rosie and a little on the stocky side.

While the adults gather for coffee on the balcony, the rest of us catch up in the living room. A lady puts out a jug filled with water, sliced lemons, and mint leaves, as well as some warm cookies.

"Thanks, Melody," Rosie says and turns to me. "She makes the most delish biscuits."

72

I take a bite. It's crunchy on the outside, chewy on the inside, and the chocolate melts on my tongue.

The twins are a few months older than me. Rosie is the oldest, but so far Rhys is the loudest. "I play rugby and football, what you call soccer, for school. Do you follow football? I think Chelsea will clinch the Premier League this year."

"Don't let my dad hear you. He's a die-hard Liverpool fan," I say. "What about you, Rosie?"

"I'm on the student council and play with the school tennis club, but ballet takes up most of my time. Dad says you play hockey."

"I can't wait to check the school team out." I gulp some lemony water. "I forgot to ask, what house are you in? I'm in Earth."

"Me, too," says Rhys. "Rosie's in Water."

"Same as me," says Millie. "What's the deal with them?"

"The five houses are named after the five Chinese elements—Metal, Earth, Water, Fire and Wood. We don't do too much with them day to day, but for big events and intramurals, we divide into house teams."

House teams: that sounds super fun and so Harry Potter–esque.

"What's that old building?" Millie asks, face against the window, pointing to the white building with the garden on the grounds of our complex.

"That's the old Repulse Bay Hotel. It used to be big with movie stars and royals back in the olden days," Rhys says.

"They do a scrummy afternoon tea. And down by the beach are some little shops and cafés. We should go after school today," Rosie says. "And if you walk farther along, there's a little temple."

"I'd love to see the temple," I say.

"Yes, Hols is hoping to get more in touch with her Chinese heritage," says Millie, laughing. I shoot her a look, and she mouths *What?*

"But that's brilliant," Rosie says, to my surprise. "The culture is so fascinating. I'm always learning new things."

"We went to Easter camp in Taipei last year to brush up on our Mandarin," Rhys says.

"You guys speak Chinese?" Millie stares in disbelief.

"Yes, Mandarin, but not much Cantonese, though. Mandarin is a required course at school," Rhys says.

"Are you kidding me?" Millie asks. "I thought I was done with that forever."

"I guess you'll be getting in touch with your Chinese heritage, too." I give her a gentle poke in the arm.

She pushes me away with a huff and asks, "More importantly, anyone rich and famous live here? There were lots of fancy cars on the podium when we walked by just now." Millie looks ready to whip out her phone for selfies with Donnie Yen from *Rogue One*. We've watched it together countless times because she has the hots for Diego Luna. But I'd love to be fierce like Jyn Erso.

"The Lo family owns the whole complex. They take up a floor of the parking garage with their Ferraris, Maseratis, and Bentleys." Rhys sounds a little awestruck.

"Who are the Los?" Millie asks.

"Lo, like in Lo Holdings?" I ask.

Rhys nods.

Millie looks puzzled.

"You know, Mom's company." The reason we're even here.

"Lofty Heights—notice the first two letters spell *Lo*?" Rhys asks.

"It's a big tycoon family. Many of them live here, mainly in the tower penthouses," Rosie says.

"Any of them our age and cute?" asks Millie, steering

75

the conversation back to what she thinks is clearly more vital information.

Before Millie gets her answer, Uncle Charlie starts telling us to grab our schoolbags, put our shoes back on, and head to the bus stop.

"The bus comes in five minutes," he announces. He told us the neighbors in Tai Tam complained that all the chauffeurs were blocking the roads at school drop-off and pickup, so now everyone needs to take the school bus.

"I can't believe we have to take a bus," I groan as I fix my ponytail for the fourth time.

"I know. What are we, six?" Millie says.

Dad starts putting his shoes on, too. "Would you like me to come with you to the bus stop?" His voice is full of hope.

I'm a little nervous about today and secretly want him to come down with us, but I'm not sure how that'll look to a bus stop full of future schoolmates.

"No, thanks, Dad. We'll be fine." We both reach over and give him a kiss and join the others out the door.

We get into the lift, and the parents send us a chorus of "Good luck!" And as the doors close, I feel like a chapter of my life is closing, and a new one is about to begin.

7

The bus pulls to a stop, and Millie and I gaze openmouthed as we step off. The school looks more amazing in person than in the photos on the website. I would be lying if I said it wasn't a little bit intimidating. It's like I stepped into ancient Greece—the building has dozens of columns, and I half expect someone to walk out in a toga. Rosie tells us it's a scaled-down replica of the British Museum. I hope I don't get lost.

Outside the school is a frenzy of motion and noise. People are greeting each other with hugs and high fives after a summer away. I hear about places like Nantucket, Niseko, and Provence as well as things like math camp, Chinese tutors, and extra-credit courses. But everyone seems warm and friendly, and I'm sure I'll fit right in.

A man dressed in a three-piece navy suit stands by the main entry, smiling and greeting students. Mr. Gregg, the head of school. I don't know how he looks so composed in this heat; he must be boiling. I catch him discreetly mopping his shiny head with a handkerchief. At that moment, a white Tesla SUV rolls up with a license plate that says GEMS. The doors open upward, like a bird about to take flight. A beautiful girl gets out. She looks so familiar, but I can't place her. She sweeps back her shiny, bouncy black hair to show off a pair of the largest diamond earrings I have ever seen. They sparkle so brightly I can see them from where I'm standing.

Mr. Gregg runs over to her car eagerly. "Welcome back, welcome back, Gemma! So lovely to see you again." He fawns over her, clapping his hands.

"I thought you said there was mandatory busing," I lean over and say to Rosie.

"There is." Rosie gives an audible sigh.

That doesn't seem fair to those that follow the rules.

"Who is she?" Millie asks.

"Gemma Tsien, queen bee of the Lower School last year," Rhys says.

"Does that mean she's in our grade?" I ask.

Rosie nods and rolls her eyes. "Mr. Gregg's always making a big deal about her. Her mother is the chair of the PTA."

Gemma takes her brown-and-gold monogrammed Louis Vuitton schoolbag from her uniformed driver. Rhys goes up to her and greets her with the same excitement as Mr. Gregg did.

Rosie shakes her head. "He follows her around like a puppy."

Two more beautiful girls arrive, and Gemma gives them both double-cheek kisses.

"Who are they?" My gaze fixes on the three of them. I remember the first day of school last year, how Natalie and I would hug and greet each other as if we hadn't just spent the entire summer together.

"Rainbow Hsieh is the one with the top bun and big hoop earrings. She's from California."

I eye her Kanken backpack, the ochre one with embroidered flowers that I saw at The Bay last month. Ah-ma promised to buy it for me as a back-to-school treat, but we were in such a rush we forgot all about it.

"And the other girl?" The one with the pink Hello Kitty backpack, which I guess is supposed to be ironic on someone who is twelve.

"That's Syut-Kei Wong. She goes by Snowy. She's from

Hong Kong, but she tells everyone she's from New York City because she lived there for a few years."

Snowy's hair is long and straight, the front pulled to the side by a pearl-covered barrette that matches her pearl-stud earrings.

"She looks very prim and proper." I eye her patent flats and their satin bows.

Rosie giggles. "She has her own YouTube channel, so she has an image to maintain."

"Is this the set of *Mean Girls*?" Millie laughs nervously.

"Don't worry. They're all pretty nice, once you get to know them. Even Gemma," Rosie says.

"We'll all be great friends before you know it," I say.

Rosie looks at me curiously. "I like your confidence, Holly-Mei."

Rosie gives us a quick tour of campus before the bell is due to ring. We climb the stairs to the roof terrace of one of the wings. Millie and I are awestruck.

"This looks like a mash-up of an Olympic training ground and a beach resort."

Tai Tam Prep has its own sandy beach and sailing club. Set back from the sea is a huge swimming pool with a retractable roof. On top of the buildings are tennis courts where students are coached by retired Grand Slam winners. Rosie says she did a clinic with Venus Williams last year. On the north side is a stadium for rugby and soccer. And what I see next to it makes my stomach flutter with excitement: a Smurf-blue pitch dedicated to field hockey. I can't wait to play on it.

"And, Millie, you'll appreciate this, the school has its own organic vegetable farm, used for both the cafeteria and the culinary club."

Millie squeals and says she can't wait to learn more.

We climb back down to the crystalline-white marble-floored main lobby, and Rosie and I say goodbye to Millie, who walks into the lower-school block. The two of us walk through to the upper-school block and look at the posted list of homerooms. Beside my name is 7A. Rosie is in 7B.

"I guess I'll see you later," I say, forcing my voice to sound cheery, even though I won't know anyone in my homeroom.

"I'll save you a seat in the cafeteria at lunch. Good luck." She gives me a quick hug before she pops into her classroom. "Yours is two doors down."

I take a deep breath and step inside. The classroom is full of students continuing their postsummer catch-ups. No one notices me, and I slip into an empty desk.

"Hey, are you Holly-Mei?" I hear someone ask.

"Yes." I look toward the desk next to mine, surprised. A cute Chinese guy smiles at me, his braces glinting.

"I'm Henry. My mate Rhys told me to look out for you," he says, still smiling.

"Hi, Henry. Nice to meet you." My shoulders relax. He seems super friendly.

But then the girl behind me clears her throat. "Sorry, that seat's taken," she says nervously.

I turn and recognize her as Snowy, the prissy one with the pearls.

"It looks pretty empty to me, Snowy," Henry says.

"I'm saving it for Gemma," she says, almost pleading.

Henry points at the dozen empty desks around. "There's plenty for her to choose from."

"But I prefer this one," someone beside me says, matter-of-factly.

I turn, and so does every other head in the room.

"Hello, Henry. The family missed you on the boat yesterday."

"Hey, Gems. I had rugby."

Gemma looks at me with arched eyebrows as I stay seated at her desk, and she starts tapping her foot.

Why does she want this stupid desk so much? There's no way I'm moving. I cross my arms and arch my eyebrows back at her.

She swooshes her hair, and then it hits me why she looks so familiar.

"Hey, we were on the same plane last week. From Toronto," I say.

I see a flash of recognition in her eyes, but then she says, "No, that wasn't me."

I'm about to insist it's her, but Henry jumps in about the desk. "Don't worry, homeroom is only ten minutes before we have to go to our next class. So it doesn't matter if you move desks."

He seems really nice, so I just go with it and move up two rows, even though it's ridiculous.

Our teacher, Ms. Chow, introduces herself. "Welcome to your first year of Upper School. This year is going to be extra special. We will be officially unveiling the new Tsien Wing." She pauses and nods in Gemma's direction, who then flashes the teacher a smug smile. "It will house state-of-the-art science and innovation laboratories as well as a new arts theater." She continues enthusiastically. "And your grade has been selected to showcase the school at the wing's opening ceremony. What an honor!"

"Showcase? What does that mean?" I whisper to the student beside me.

And as if Ms. Chow could hear me, she says, "You'll get more details in the coming weeks."

The rest of the morning goes pretty smoothly. Teachers and students are friendly, and classes sound pretty interesting. I can't wait for lunch so I can catch up with Rosie.

The cafeteria is humming, and I stand back to soak it all in. There are a quite a few white students, but the majority of the students look Asian or mixed-Asian. I've never seen so many people that look like me. The students' accents are either British or North American, and some a blend of the two. There is a table of kids talking about Fortnite, a table full of students wearing matching Tai Tam Dragons Volleyball hoodies, and a table of girls with matching charcoal-and-copper-striped sneakers gushing about the latest anime series. But with everybody in a uniform, it seems like a really happy, harmonious mix.

Rosie waves and calls to me from the tree-filled atrium area where she has a table with a few of the people I met this morning. I'm surprised to see Gemma there. I didn't get the vibe that they were good friends. Maybe they're more frenemies. I make a mental note to ask her later. Even I know not to ask that in front of everyone. Apart from Rosie and Rhys, the table is a sea of Asian and mixed faces. Rhys and some of the guys greet each other with a postsummer bro hug, a combination handshake and one-armed hug, which ends by slapping each other on the back. I meet Jinsae Kim, a cute Korean boy who plays rugby with Henry and Rhys. I'm also introduced to Rainbow, the girl with the hoops, who smiles warmly at me. I hear chatter about rugby and field hockey, as well as grumblings about homework already assigned.

Rosie and I line up with our trays at the food counter.

"So how was your morning?" Rosie asks.

"Good. I met some nice people, including a friend of Rhys's, Henry."

I see a light shade of pink slide across Rosie's cheeks. "Yes, Henry is very nice. Henry Lo."

"Like the Lo family that Rhys mentioned?"

"Yes, he lives at the top of our tower. He's super friendly. Last year we were on the Battle of the Books team together."

"Who's that he's with?" I ask, spying Henry walking toward our table with a tall boy in a red hoodie.

"That's Theo, Henry's cousin. Theo Fitzwilliam-Lo," Rhys says, jumping into line behind us. "We play rugby together."

"He lives in the top flat of your tower," Rosie says.

"For his birthday party last year, his dad booked out all of Hong Kong Disneyland just for us. It was so much fun," Rhys says.

I wonder if this is the same Fitzwilliam family from the shipping company Mom mentioned on the ride from the airport.

When I get to the front of the line, or *queue* as Rosie calls it, there are no egg salad or tuna mayo sandwiches in sight, although there are some baguettes with brie and Iberico ham. It's the hot section that gets my mouth watering. Miso ramen noodles, tempura bento boxes, barbecue pork with rice, pan-fried dumplings—I don't know what to choose. I go for braised tofu and eggplant with jasmine rice; Rosie gets ramen with tempura shrimp. We grab some chopsticks and quickly head back to our table. I can't wait to devour this feast. Rhys stays behind to wait for his wood-fired pizza.

When we get back to our seats, Henry is at the table. I make sure I leave room so Rosie can sit next to him.

"Hi, Henry. You know my cousin Holly-Mei."

"Yes, we met in homeroom. She hit it off smashingly with Gemma. They'll be best friends in no time."

"Really?" Rosie asks.

"No." I laugh. "I don't think there's a chance of that anytime soon." But I don't care: there are so many other great people to become friends with here, there's no need to think twice about someone who's so precious about a desk.

"Gemma's like a turtle. Hard on the outside but soft under her shell." Henry glances over to where she's sitting. "Our families have been friends for ages."

Rhys looks over at Gemma, and his eyes twinkle. "She's really cool, you'll see. Rosie, remember in kinder-garten, her dad came in dressed as Santa and gave us all these remote-controlled cars and talking dolls?" With a mouthful of pizza, he says, "They have a huge toy factory."

"And her mother used to be a Hong Kong film star. She was in that Bruce Lee biopic."

Dad loves Bruce Lee. I'm going to ask him if we can watch that movie together.

After eating, I get up to refill my glass at the water station. The guy in front of me, in a Tai Tam Dragons Rugby hoodie, is balancing a tray in one hand and is trying to fill his glass with the other. His tray wobbles, and I can't bear to see his bento box crash to the floor, so I step forward and move to grab it. But I'm half a second too late, and it starts tipping in slow motion. He looks at me, eyes wide, as pieces of ginger, salmon, and rice fly through the air. He deftly moves the tray and catches everything, like it was all part of a successful circus act. Even his glass of water hasn't spilled. He smiles proudly, but then his smile suddenly disappears as he looks at my shirt.

"Oh my God. I'm so, so sorry," he says. He puts down his tray and hands me a napkin.

I look down and my new white uniform has a neon-pink stain at the front, and there's a piece of pickled beetroot at my feet. I try and wipe it, but the pink circle just grows, making him apologize even more profusely. I offer a shrug and say, "Don't worry, I like pink anyway."

"I'm sure it'll come out. Give me your shirt, and I'll get it cleaned."

I wish I could do that one-raised-eyebrow thing like Mom and Ah-ma. Instead, I say, "Excuse me?"

"I mean, do you have an extra top? To wear while I take this one. Or we can go to the uniform shop and get a new one."

"Don't worry. I'll put some lemon juice on it at home. I'm sure it'll come out," I say reassuringly.

He runs his hand through his dark wavy hair. I feel bad that he's so concerned. It's kind of cute. He's kind of cute. He's Eurasian, mixed-Asian like me. Takes one to know one, I think.

"I'm Theo."

"I'm Holly-Mei. Hey, you're Henry's cousin, right? I'm Rosie and Rhys's cousin."

I fill up my water, and as we walk back to the table together, he asks me about the move.

"It must have been hard leaving all your friends."

"I'm just excited for my new Hong Kong adventure."

I sit back down beside Rosie, and he moves to the end to join Rhys and Jinsae. I hear greetings of "Hey, Fitzy." I also notice Gemma looking over at me curiously.

Last period of the day is French, which should be a breeze. I'm in the advanced class since I've been taking French since kindergarten. I walk into the classroom but stop at the doorway when I see Gemma and Theo just in front of me. I wait for her to take a seat—beside him, of course—before choosing one just behind them. I wouldn't want to get kicked out of my desk again. I do a mental eye roll as I think back to the morning.

"Theo, remember when our families met up in Paris last summer?" Gemma asks, leaning over in his direction.

"Yes." Theo doesn't look up from his copy of the green Bescherelle grammar guide, which is covered with colorful Post-it tabs.

"Wasn't Disneyland Paris so much fun?"

"Uh-huh."

"Which is your favorite Disney? I've been to all of them. Obviously, Disney World is the biggest. But I think the one in Paris is my favorite. The snacks! Marshmallow Mickey and Nutella crepes."

Gemma looks over at me then and leans even farther toward Theo. I'm afraid she's going to fall out of her chair.

"And I just loved our day at the Louvre Museum, didn't you? My favorite was the Delacroix painting, *Viva la Vida*."

I let out a huge laugh. She's talking about the *Liberty Leading the People* painting that's on the Coldplay album cover. Dad and I watched a documentary about how the painting influenced Victor Hugo to write *Les Misérables*. Theo is trying to muffle a laugh, dimples on show. Gemma's eyes shoot arrows at me.

She turns to me and says, "And what's your favorite part of Paris?"

"I've never been," I say.

"No, of course you haven't," she says with a smirk and continues to talk about all the different Disneylands she's been to.

I shrug it off. She's the one that made the dumb mistake.

After the school bell rings for the end of the first day, Theo turns to me and says, "You should sign up for the school hiking club. It's a great way to see the beauty of Hong Kong. Our first hike is this Saturday." I glow inside at his niceness.

And just like that, I've added hiking to my list of extracurriculars at Tai Tam Prep.

8

The selection of chocolate bars at the grocery store by the foot of our building looks jaw-droppingly delicious. I grab a green-tea Kit Kat for Millie and a salt-lychee Kit Kat for myself. These should give us enough energy for our excursion with the school hiking club this morning. They hike one Saturday a month. I can't wait to get moving and do some exercise after being cooped up at school all week.

I take the lift back upstairs, and when the doors open at my floor, a tall lady with long brown hair and golden highlights is waiting to get in. She's dressed like she's on her way to the gym, even though her hair looks freshly blow-dried and she smells like a department-store perfume counter.

"Good morning," she says.

"Hi," I say, unsure who she is.

She stands halfway in the hall and halfway in the lift, so the doors can't close.

"I'm Tinsley Rosenblum from 28A. Are you from the new family in 28B?" she asks in a slight American twang.

"Oh, yes. Hi, I'm Holly-Mei. We just moved from Toronto." I take a step toward my front door.

"Welcome to Hong Kong. I'm friends with your aunt Helen. My husband Ken's bank does business with your mother's company. Tell her I'll organize a dinner party soon," she says. It seems like everyone knows each other's business here. Without taking a breath, she continues, "Where are you going to school? The Canadian school? It has a very good reputation."

"My sister and I just started at Tai Tam Prep."

"Oh, you can't get a better school than Tai Tam Prep," she says. "My daughter, Aisling, just graduated from there and is about to start Princeton."

"Oh, wow." I don't know much about Princeton, but the way she says it makes it clear I should be impressed.

Before Tinsley can continue speaking, the alarm in the lift beeps.

"Oh, that's my signal to go down. I must get to yoga. I have a private class booked. Don't forget to tell your mother I'll be in touch." She smiles, her perfect white teeth flashing like a strobe light, and waves as the lift doors shut.

As soon as I walk in the front door, Millie reaches for my shopping bag and opens the Kit Kat, munching right away.

"Hey, that's for the hike," I say.

"I'm hungry now," she says as she walks away toward the kitchen.

"Who were you talking to outside?" Mom asks, looking up from her newspaper. She and Dad are having their usual leisurely Saturday read over breakfast.

"The lady next door. She said she'd be in touch." I shrug at Dad's inquiring eyes. "Something about having us over for dinner." I grab the leftover crust from Mom's toast and pop it in my mouth. Mom nods like she was expecting the invitation.

"You girls sure about this hike? There's teacher supervision, right?" Mom asks.

"It's awfully hot outside," Dad says.

"Yes, for the hundredth time, we'll be fine," I say. Each morning, I've looked out my bedroom window at those leafy green hills and imagined how beautiful they must be. I am bursting to get outside.

"And don't forget to put on sunscreen. I bought you some SPF 90 cream. Extra attention on your face, please. You're already quite tanned," Mom says. She must see my grimace, because she says, "You'll thank me when you don't have wrinkles later."

In front of the bathroom mirror, with resentful strokes, I slather the coconut-smelling sunscreen all over my face.

As we step out the door, Mom yells out, "Hats, girls!"

"Yeah, yeah," we yell back in unison.

"And go have fun," Mom says as the lift doors close on us.

We meet the twins in the lobby, and we talk animatedly about the hike, but Millie changes her mind about coming the second we step out the door and into the sauna-level heat.

"It's too hooot," she whines and fans herself with her hat in an exaggerated motion.

I pull at my sports bra to loosen the little pool of sweat already forming. Rhys convinces Millie it won't be too bad once we are near enough to feel the breeze from the sea. Ramon, their driver, pulls up, and we jump into the van to meet the rest of the group at the hike starting point.

"I hope you've packed enough water," Rhys says.

"Two bottles and some chocolate to share," I say. Although I'm not sure a chocolate bar is going to survive in solid form in this heat.

We drive by a group of ladies walking down to the beach with their giant welderlike visor hats on. Those can't be for keeping cool. It must be to keep from getting tanned and dark. They are even wearing gloves to protect their hands. I can't imagine wearing any extra clothes in this weather. I wonder if they've been reading those same magazines with the whitening-cream ads.

The van winds along the same road we take to school. I could almost imagine we're on some deserted tropical island if it weren't for the buildings. Some are plain apartment blocks surrounded by palm trees. Some are mini-palaces inside ornate gates painted gold.

"Wow, everything is so different on the South Side," I say. "On the drive from the airport, there were so many buildings all one on top of another, but it's so peaceful here."

"We need to take you to Stanley." Rosie points to the village by the sea. "There's a burger place along the boardwalk, a great bubble tea shop, and a cute little market."

"Oh, shopping! Can we do that instead of hiking?" Millie asks. "I'm not sure I want to be part of this hiking club. Why did I let you drag me?"

"Henry said his sister Lizzie was coming. She's in your grade. Maybe you can make a friend," I say.

Millie looks wounded. I'm more surprised than she is that she hasn't found a group to gel with yet. I guess I have Rosie and Rhys in my grade, so it makes it easier. I'm hoping she and Lizzie will hit it off.

Rhys points to the water. "At Stanley Main Beach, you can rent kayaks and stand-up paddleboards. And dragon boating starts in the spring."

"That sounds so cool," I say. I'm totally going to try that. I can imagine the *boom boom boom* of the dragon-boat drummer pushing the paddlers to go faster.

"And surfing?" Millie asks with a speck of hope in her voice.

"You'd have to go to Big Wave Bay for that. We'll end our hike there today."

"Fantastic." Millie's voice chirps up, and she's suddenly sounding enthused for today's outing.

After a few more twists and turns, we pass Tai Tam

Prep on a hill to the right. The school's columns gleam in the sunshine. Even though it's what Dad called *a top private school*, everyone seems superfriendly and not concerned about being fancy. Mom was wrong to worry about *the right people*. I feel so lucky to go there. And last night, Rosie told me that Luciana Aymar, eight-time winner of the world's best field hockey player title, was a guest coach for the school team last year. I cross my fingers and hope that, if I make the team, she'll come and coach again this year.

We drive over a sandstone-colored reservoir dam that looks like an old Roman bridge and enter the country park, going farther away from any buildings or signs of city life. Ramon drops us off in what seems like the middle of nowhere.

"We're getting out here?" Millie asks, sounding skeptical.

"It's the start of the Dragon's Back Trail," Rhys says.

We greet the group of thirty or so students standing to the edge of the road and wait for a few more to arrive. Most people I don't recognize, but I do see Theo and Gemma chatting at one end of the group. Mr. Chapman, one of the PE teachers, leads a round of introductions, and then he leads us up a single-track path.

There's a trail marker along the road with a carved

dragon painted in orange, white, and yellow, pointing us in the direction of some stairs. Despite the early morning, the sun is strong and beating down on us. I grudgingly concede that Mom was right about the need to wear a hat.

After about twenty minutes of straight vertical, we reach a peak with a bench.

"Thank God we're done," Millie says. She has her hands on her knees, panting.

Rhys laughs. "Millie, this is just the beginning. We have another two hours to go."

"They call it the Dragon's Back because the trail curves like the back of the dragon," Rosie says as she points to the trail along the ridge. I imagine Sisu from *Raya and the Last Dragon* as she moves across the sky. The view is amazing: green hills on one side and the big wide ocean on the other.

"After the last peak, we head down and end up at Big Wave Bay Beach," Henry says. He seemingly popped out of nowhere to start walking beside us. He introduces Millie and Lizzie, and after a few awkward smiles, Lizzie pushes her glasses up her nose and offers a bunch of green-tea Pocky sticks to Millie. As we walk, I can hear the two of them start chatting about chocolate, cooking, and all the surfers they will see later today.

"What's that beach down there?" I point to the beach right below us.

"That's Shek O," says Rhys.

I make out lifeguard huts and a couple of yellow and red sun umbrellas set up on the sand. Just like in Repulse Bay, there are pontoons out in the water, but we're too far away to see any swimmers. The village is full of little colorful houses all clustered together, the polar opposite of the city center.

"And that," Rhys says, pointing to a bright green fairway farther along the coast, "is the Shek O golf course and country club."

I wonder how many golf balls get lost in the sea. "Whoa, nice houses!" Huge mansions dot the outer edges of the golf course.

"Do you see that one there? That is Gemma Tsien's house," Rosie whispers.

I suck in my breath. *House* is not really the word I'd use to describe the golden limestone structure. It has a wall of arched windows interlaced with columns. It seems a little OTT. "They sure do like their columns here." There's even a fountain flanked by ornately designed symmetrical gardens.

"They named it Petit Versailles," Rosie says playfully, but with an edge. I giggle at the fact her house has a name.

I've seen images online of Versailles, the opulent palace built by Louis XIV just outside of Paris. Gemma Tsien, Tai Tam Prep's very own Marie Antoinette.

"You sound like you have some history with her. Spill the tea." I nudge Rosie gently with my elbow.

"Rosie's still bitter she lost out to Gemma for the role of Clara in *The Nutcracker* last year," Rhys says.

She looks around to make sure no one else is listening. "She used to dance with me at the City Ballet Youth Academy. Her mother is a patron. I guess I shouldn't have expected anything different," Rosie says. "Gemma likes to get what Gemma wants."

I kind of got that impression already, starting with our first encounter in homeroom.

We stop for a water break, which can't come soon enough. I drink so fast, half of it dribbles down my shirt. Just my luck, that's when Theo comes up to me.

"How do you like Hong Kong so far?" he asks warmly.

"It's amazing. But OMG, so hot!" I say, and I finish off one of my water bottles. "No wonder my Ah-ma, my grandmother, said it was too hot for her."

"Ah-ma? Do you have Chinese heritage?" he asks.

I nod. "My mom's originally from Taiwan. My dad's English. How'd you guess?"

He smiles and says, "Takes one," and I chime in, "to know one." We both laugh.

"My dad's family is Chinese, and my mom's family is Scottish, but both families have been in Hong Kong for ages."

"You must have amazing stories to tell about the city." I leave out questions about Scottish pirates, in case Dad was pulling my leg.

"Anything you really miss about Canada?"

"Just Ah-ma."

He nods thoughtfully. "I'm really lucky my grandmother lives with us. I call her maa maa. That's *grandmother, father's mother*, in Cantonese."

"Want to teach me some? I figure I better learn a few words," I say.

He smiles and says, "For sure." He starts counting, "Yat, yi, sam, sei, mm. *One, two, three, four, five.*"

"Oh, that's confusing. Yi is the number *one* in Mandarin but the number *two* in Cantonese?" I rub my forehead.

"You'll get used to it. Ok, here's an easy one. Joh-sun means *good morning.*"

"Joh-sun. Got it. Sun, as in the morning sun. I can handle that."

He flashes a smile, and my stomach flutters unexpectedly when I see his deep dimples.

Theo suddenly turns away. Someone has grabbed his arm. It's Gemma, out of breath, like she ran to catch up.

"Theo, Holly-Mei, wait up. You are walking so quickly," she says between pants. "Holly-Mei is so much more sporty than me."

I'm pleased with her compliment.

"What are you two talking and laughing about? Fill me in on all the secrets," she says.

"No secrets," I say. "Theo's just teaching me some Cantonese."

"Oh, that's so charming. Well, don't forget about mm goi. It's the most useful word ever. It means *excuse me, please*, and *thank you*, all rolled into one word."

"Oh, cool. Thanks, Gemma." I practice saying mm goi under my breath.

"Anytime, Holly-Mei. Anything you need, let me know," she says, locking her arm into mine, her voice as sweet as honey.

She's been gradually nicer and nicer to me all week. I guess Henry was right: she is really nice under her hard shell. Maybe we'll end up being supertight friends.

I am amazed by my lush surroundings, like a sanctuary just minutes from our flat. There are no buildings in sight, except for the mansions below, and no people, except for the few hiking in the distance ahead and a couple of paragliders in the sky. As we walk, I take a long, deep breath, and I feel energized. Especially as I think about all the new friends I'm making.

We come to the last peak of the trail, and Rhys points out Big Wave Bay Beach in the distance.

"That's where we end the hike. If you fancy surfing, this is the best place to do it in Hong Kong," Rhys says.

"Oh, surfers!" Millie points excitedly to the people surfing in the small bay, and she and Lizzie huddle in fits of giggles.

Mr. Chapman gives them an odd look. She laughs it off and pretends she's joking, but I won't be surprised if she picks up surfing just to check the guys out.

"The trail goes down through the forest, and we'll end up on the beach soon," Rosie says.

When we reach Big Wave Bay village, the teacher announces, "Kids, you are free to make your way around here for lunch or head home, but don't leave without letting me know."

A bunch of us agree to eat at the nearby noodle shack and then hang out on the beach afterward. I sit down at the big round communal table and sip the last drops of my water as I wait for my lunch. Theo and Henry join me when they're done ordering, and we chat about what other hikes the club is planning on doing this year.

Gemma announces her arrival at the table by squeezing a chair in between me and Theo.

"Holly-Mei, since you are trying to go local, here is a drink you have to try," she says as she places a can of Schweppes cream soda in front of me.

"Oh, thanks. I've had cream soda before."

"Not like this, you haven't," she says as she pours the bubbly contents of the can into a cup. Then she proceeds to pour some milk into it.

"Stop! What are you doing?" I ask, a little grossed out.

"Trust her. It's so good," Theo says.

Gemma flicks her hair and flashes him a huge grin.

I scrunch my nose at the concoction. "Really?"

"Really," Henry says.

"You're not pranking me?"

"No, I would never do that," Gemma says in mock offense.

I look for Rosie to get her opinion on the bubbly white drink, but she is still at the counter ordering lunch.

"Okay, fine," I say as I close my eyes and take a sip. My eyes go wide as I get a mouthful of magic. "This is so good!" I say and take another huge gulp.

"I told you. I would never do anything to trick you,"

Gemma says as she pats my hand. "Oh, before I forget, you and your family have to make sure you come to mine next Friday night. My family is hosting a welcome party for new families at our house. You might have seen it on the hike. Petit Versailles?"

"Really? That's so cool. For sure, we'll be there." I smile warmly at her. I've been here just over a week, and I've already been invited to my first party, at my new friend Gemma's house. I don't know what Ah-ma was on about, with all her talk of bitterness. Life right now is as sweet as my milky cream soda.

9

It's Friday, the night of the Tai Tam Prep New Families' Welcome Party, an event hosted at the beginning of every school year by Reina Leung and Godwin Tsien, Gemma's parents. I can't wait to see Gemma's house, or rather mansion, Petit Versailles, up close. Our apartment is full of energy and nervous excitement, and even Mom and Dad were muttering about the *Hong Kong elite*.

Dad is in the hallway talking with Mom. "Darling, you know how uncomfortable I am making small talk with strangers at parties. I'd much prefer to stay home and read a book."

"I know you hate these kinds of things, honey," Mom says, and she touches his arm, "but there are many execs who will be there with their families, and I want to give a good impression. If the small talk leads to forming new friendships tonight, it would mean a lot."

Dad wraps his arms around her. "You've worked so hard. I won't let you down."

"I'm just relieved it's paying off." Mom lets out a long sigh. "If it amounted to nothing, every missed parent-teacher meeting or field hockey game or take-out dinner at my desk would just hurt more."

"Got it. I'll go change," Dad says, and he kisses Mom and walks into their room.

I never knew Mom felt guilty about missing those things. I walk up and reach for her hand. She lifts it and gives it a quick kiss before saying with a smile, "Now, go get ready, Holly-Mei. We're leaving in an hour."

I throw the contents of my drawers on my bed. I hold up my trusty T-shirt dress to the mirror and decide against it. I want to look a little nicer tonight. Even though Theo and Henry aren't new students, Gemma has invited them, along with the usual gang. "Host's prerogative," she said. This is a big occasion—my first party in Hong Kong, the first of many with my new friends. At the thought of the word *friends*, the image of Natalie's face flashes in my head, and I can't help but reach for my phone and flip through her Insta stories, getting sucked into a vortex of videos of her, Katie, and Ellie smiling and laughing. But who needs them now, I think as I toss my phone down on my bed.

I hear Mom yell, "Ten minutes," and I start to search frantically through my pile of clothes.

Mom calls me into her bedroom.

"Holly-Mei, let me see what you are wearing." Mom is in front of the mirror arguing with my sister.

"Amelia-Tian Jones, you are not thinking of wearing that, are you?" My mother glares at Millie's cropped T-shirt and denim skirt, frayed around the edges.

"Mom, it's so hot out, I don't want to wear any more clothes. It's too uncomfortable!"

"Can you find something a bit more classy? That outfit makes me look like a bad mother."

I initially laugh at the notion that something as trivial as an outfit can impact how people at this party will think of my mom. But then my laughter stops short. Will this crowd be judging her by how we behave? How we dress? Is this why she's so nervous?

Mom looks me up and down. "That looks fine." She gives a curt nod of approval.

111

I'm wearing my silver star-shaped stud earrings and a gray linen shirt dress that goes down to my knees, a hand-me-down from Rosie. She said it was Japanese chic. Simple, yet elegant, but just not her color.

"Although you could make more of an effort with your hair," she says, to my surprise. "Can you leave it down instead of having it up in a ponytail? You look like you're on your way to PE class. And wear my red earrings for a pop of color."

Millie and I look at each other with alarm. Mom has never commented on how we look and never encouraged us to care about clothes. She used to say that concerning ourselves with our looks was shallow and distracted us from important things, like school and grades. Mom seems more nervous than us about this party.

She motions to Millie and me to sit on the bed, and she pulls up a chair so that we're eye-level.

"Tonight is very important," she says. "This is not just any party. This is your introduction to the social scene at Tai Tam Prep. Very prominent and influential people will be there tonight, including senior admin from your school, senior members of my company, and as a matter of fact, senior members of Hong Kong society. Their children go to school with you, and it's not only important for me to make connections, but for you as well."

We don't dare say anything and just nod robotically.

"Millie, you're bubbly, but sometimes you can be a bit loud. Try and keep your volume down. Remember your indoor voice. And, Holly-Mei—" Mom lets out a little sigh "—you have a tendency to blurt out what you're thinking. Remember to filter, okay?"

"Sure," Millie and I say.

"Guanxi, my darlings, is the Chinese word for *connections*, but it's so much deeper than that. It's not just knowing someone. It's about trust and loyalty. Opportunity." She looks at us both, taking our silence for agreement, and she smiles.

"Now, go finish up." She pats us on the legs before walking into her bathroom.

My sister and I remain on the bed, unsure of what has just happened.

We arrive—I, wearing mom's red earrings and a pair of her ballet flats, and Millie, still in her crop top, but with a black miniskirt instead of the denim one, and her leopard-print flats. I'm even wearing pink lip gloss that Millie helped me apply from her secret stash. We are greeted by uniformed men and women who usher us through a reception room into the back garden, where we are promptly offered tiny crackers topped with mounds of little black balls.

"Yuck," I whisper. "So salty." I wipe my tongue discreetly on a napkin.

"It's caviar. It's supposed to be salty," Millie says, giggling.

Mom's eyes widen. She turns a pretend volume dial down with her hand. "Go find some of your school friends," she says through a forced smile, "and please behave."

While Mom and Dad stop to talk to people, Millie and I go exploring. A fountain in the middle of the yard has a huge golden Chinese dragon statue standing on white marble clouds.

"Doesn't this look like it should be in the lobby of Yangtze?" Millie says, referring to our favorite Chinese restaurant back home. I giggle and shush her.

There are even larger-than-life topiaries of panda bears. "Look, it's Po from *Kung Fu Panda*." I pretend to do a front kick and end up narrowly missing Millie. "Oops," I say when she shoots me a look.

"Whoa, look at that pool," she says, pulling my arm. The infinity pool seems to end in the ocean, as if the water is falling over the edge of the horizon.

"What do you think is in there?" she asks, pointing to a white marquee.

"Food tent!" I say, and we hurry inside. It's full of people already. The tent buzzes with chatter, and violinists from the school orchestra play classical music in the background. I turn around when I hear *pop!* Someone has opened a bottle of champagne, and it's foaming over.

"Oh my," says Millie, gushing over the lobster mac and cheese and truffle fries in the big silver dishes on the buffet table. My eyes go wide at the sushi display, and I pop a piece of spicy salmon maki into my mouth. There is another table for desserts, including chocolate cupcakes and tarts topped with fresh raspberries. I'm most excited to see a fountain, taller than me, flowing with white, milk, and dark chocolate, with sticks of fruit and marshmallows nearby for dipping.

"What was Mom saying about all that guanxi stuff?" Millie asks as she attempts to stick her finger into the white-chocolate waterfall.

I knock her hand away. "I'm sure it's nothing we need

to worry about," I say as I grab two fresh lime sodas from a rotating waiter. I pass her one and say, "Let's go find Gemma and Rosie."

I stop outside the tent and look at the people milling around on the lawn, trying to spot someone I recognize. Mom is talking to Mr. Gregg, who is wearing the same three-piece suit he wore on the first day of school. Probably not a good idea, because he's already dabbing his forehead with his handkerchief—even though it's evening, it's still hot and humid. Mom nods in our direction and points over to a group of students across the lawn. I recognize them as part of the Tai Tam Prep student council from the school newsletter. Millie and I walk over, and a pretty girl with trendy black-rimmed glasses starts speaking.

"Hi, welcome, everyone. I'm Scholastica Chang, Grade 7 student council rep. I've been lucky to have attended Tai Tam Prep since kindergarten. I'm also the captain of the junior field hockey team and a member of the Habitat for Humanity club. My dad is from Hong Kong, and my mom's from Ireland, hence the strong ginger genes," she laughs as she points to her thick wavy auburn locks.

As Scholastica continues to talk about the different clubs and activities new students can get involved in, I can't help but stare at her in wonderment. I would never have guessed she was mixed-Asian with her hair the color of red velvet cake and freckles to match, except for her beautifully shaped Asian eyes. I guess her name also gives it away. I wonder if she feels pressure to live up to her name. Could you be a slacker and still be named Scholastica? I guess that there are no defined boxes when it comes to the variation in people's looks or experiences. And it feels pretty cool to be connected to her somehow in our Eurasian-ness.

Scholastica nods at me, and I start to introduce myself. "Hey, I'm Holly-Mei Jones. I'm in Grade 7, and my sister, Millie, and I just moved here from Canada." The other students seem really interested in getting to know us. They ask us lots of questions like, "Is winter really six months long?" Yes. "Have you ever been to a Toronto Maple Leafs game?" No. "Justin Bieber or Shawn Mendes?" Millie says, "Justin" at the same time as I say, "Shawn."

The others go around, saying who they are and where they're from. I know a handful of boys and girls from class. Some students have transferred from other schools in Hong Kong, and some have recently moved from abroad, just like us. We've all just started talking about our first impressions of Tai Tam Prep when Millie elbows me hard in the ribs.

"What the—?"

"No, look," she whispers. "Mom's coming."

I glance behind us and see her striding over. She has the same look in her eyes that she had when talking about guanxi earlier, and I groan out loud at the thought of what she'll say in front of this group.

"Exactly," Millie says as if reading my mind.

"Good evening. I'm Holly-Mei and Amelia-Tian's mother, Gracie Li-Jones," she says so formally. "How are you all enjoying the curriculum at Tai Tam Prep so far?"

A few kids mumble something monosyllabic, but most just stare. Only Scholastica steps up and gives a gushy answer about academic excellence.

"Lovely," Mom says after a beat, a smile across her face. "Holly-Mei? Amelia-Tian? May I speak with you two privately?"

We step away from the group, and Mom leads us to the edge of the pool so her voice is masked by the sound of rushing water.

"Have you met the daughter of the people hosting us?" she asks expectantly.

"Yes, Gemma. We're friends," I say.

"Oh, good. That is welcome news," Mom says, nodding.

"Why?" Millie asks.

"Her mother is an important and well-connected woman. If you make a good impression on her, you will have hit the guanxi jackpot." An image of a slot machine ringing with a line of Gemma's face pops in my head.

"Why should we care about that?" I ask.

Millie makes silly faces behind Mom, sticking her nose in the air, snoblike.

"It's useful to have well-connected friends in this city. Who knows, maybe she can open doors for you. Anyways, I'm pleased to hear you are already friends with her daughter, Emma."

"Mom, it's *Gemma*, not *Emma*," I say. I'm shocked to hear my mom talk about how a friend could be "useful." She's never talked about connections or opportunities before. It's like coming to Hong Kong has changed things not only for us, but for her, too.

Mom walks away, waving to someone I don't know. Dad is standing just outside the food tent doing his best to listen to the woman droning away next to him. She is wearing head-to-toe Chanel, with big gold interlocking Cs on her shirt, and holding a folder with the school logo embossed on the front. I catch his eye and give a smile and a wave. At least he's not shy about hitting the buffet—his plate is filled sky-high.

Millie sees some people in her grade, and I go in search of Gemma. I walk through the garden and stop to smell the sweet peachy-scented flowers. I feel like I'm in a botanical garden, not someone's backyard. Gemma's parents must really be fancy. At the edge of the garden, I see two people talking. When I realize it's Gemma and Theo, I call out, "Hi, guys! I hope I'm not disturbing you."

"Hey, Holly-Mei, of course not." Theo leans over and gives me a double-cheek kiss. My first one ever. My cheeks are flaming hot where his cheeks met mine. I resist the urge to touch my face.

"We were just talking," Gemma says, reaching over to give me air-kisses, our cheeks inches away. "I've been looking for you everywhere. Where have you been?" She shakes her finger at me jokingly.

"I've either been in the food tent or lost in your garden," I say, laughing.

Gemma gives a sly smile. She stands between me

and Theo, links her arms with ours, and leads us back to the party.

I see Rosie, and I run over to give her a big hug. After we catch up with the others, I lead her to the marquee to check out all the amazing food. Two trips to the buffet later, we lean back in our chairs, bellies full. Gemma comes over with a plate of rainbow-colored cookies.

"Holly-Mei, you just have to try these."

"Oh, I couldn't. I've already had five chocolate-covered marshmallows."

"Oh, but you must. These are Ladurée macarons. They're completely divine. Mummy had them flown in from Paris just for the party."

"Well, then, I can't say no, can I?" I laugh as I take a pastel-pink one off her plate. It's featherlight and delicate, like a meringue, and it tastes sweet with a hint of rose, or what I imagine a rose would taste like, having never eaten one before. "Wow, this is delicious."

"Go on, have another one." Gemma pulls out her camera and takes aim. "Give me a smile."

I take two violet ones that smell like black currant and put them against my cheeks. Gemma snaps a photo.

"I dare you to put the whole plate of them in your mouth Holly-Mei," she says.

Rosie gasps.

"No way," I say, laughing.

"Come on, it'll be fun," Gemma says. "Please?"

"I can eat one more, but then I'll burst," I say, putting the violet ones inside my cheeks then take a last macaron, a cream-colored vanilla-scented one between my teeth, and I puff my cheeks out so I look like a squirrel hoarding nuts for winter. Rosie reaches for a chocolate one, which she nibbles mouselike, and we both bend over laughing. We don't even notice when Gemma walks away.

We hear the sound of glass tinkling: someone is getting prepared to make a speech, and we all move closer to the house. The woman standing on the terrace step tapping her champagne glass with a silver spoon must be Gemma's mother, Reina. She looks every bit the movie star. Dressed in a royal blue cheongsam, a traditional silk Chinese dress, her skin glows like she's under a spotlight.

"Friends," she says with a cut-glass accent, "we are so privileged to host the New Families' Welcome Party here at our humble home." I can't help but roll my eyes as I survey the *humble home* and vast grounds. She continues with a few words on the importance of education and helping children achieve the highest standard, saluting Mr. Gregg with a raised glass. Everyone else follows suit while Mr. Gregg beams and waves like a member of the royal family.

"This coming year is very auspicious. It's not only the eighty-eighth anniversary of the founding of Tai Tam Prep," she says proudly, "but it also marks the unveiling of the new Tsien Wing." The crowd breaks into rapturous applause. "This will further make Tai Tam Prep the envy of Asia, if not the world. We invite you all to attend the opening gala in the new Performing Arts Center in a few weeks. And my dear Gemma's grade will be leading the ceremonies on behalf of the school."

Oohs, aahs, and excited whispers fill the air. I guess this exhibition is a going to be a huge deal if all these people will be there.

"Here is a short film about the construction of the wing," she says as images begin to play on the screen beside her, starting with the digging of the foundation followed by time-lapse images of the building going up bit by bit, ending with the gleaming brick and glass structure, which stands imposingly on the campus. More clapping and cheers ensue from the crowd. "And here are some of the Grade 7 students who will graciously lead the opening ceremony." Images of familiar faces collecting certificates, ribbons, and trophies fill the screen. More applause. Then laughter. Lots of laughter. Laughter directed at the huge face on the screen. My face. My face, exponentially enlarged on the screen, my cheeks puffed out and a macaron between my teeth. But worse, it's not a still image. It's a Boomerang video, so it looks like I'm puffing and unpuffing my cheeks on repeat. The crowd turns in my direction, fingers point, voices cackle. My cheeks burn red-hot, and my stomach lurches. I see my mother shaking her head in disappointment. Her gaze meets mine. She looks more ashamed than angry. Gemma is smiling smugly and, when we lock eyes, puffing her cheeks.

I need to get out of here. I've become the joke of the party. I can't face Rosie and Rhys, and I certainly can't face Theo. Why would Gemma do this? I thought she was my friend. Unless she was faking being my friend the whole time?

I make a beeline for the exit. Millie grabs my arms and asks me if I'm okay, but I shake her off. I get out to the driveway and find our van. Ah-Lok, our driver, is outside chatting with the other drivers. He opens the door of the van for me, and I sit in the back corner, wishing this night were just a bad dream. I can't believe I doubted Ah-ma. She said things would be tough to start, but I bet even she never imagined having to deal with someone like Gemma Tsien, seemingly sweet like chocolate but bitter like raw cocoa.

10

The next morning I'm up before everyone. Flashbacks of last night's fiasco play over and over in my head: my Boomerang cheeks, Mom's fallen face, the laughter. I hope I haven't become some sort of meme. I shudder at the thought. I decide to take a walk along the beach and leave a note so no one worries.

It's early enough that the air is nice and fresh. The cold waves on my bare feet are relaxing. Flip-flops in hand, I walk along the wet sand. I look up to Lofty Heights and imagine the dragon flying down. I wish it would pick me up and take me away. At the far end of the beach, I see pink, blue, and yellow statues of deities. This must be the temple. The sign in front tells me that it's dedicated to Tin

Hau, the goddess that protects fishermen and those that live by the sea. Inside, it's dark, the ceilings are low, and the walls are painted red. The only sound is the ripping of paper as an elderly couple open their pack of incense. They light the sticks, bow several times, and say some prayers. The fragrant smoke swirls around them. I reach into my pocket and pull out some coins, which make a loud clanging sound as I drop them in the donation box. The temple caretaker gives me some incense sticks, which I light with fire from a silver bowl. They burst into flames before settling into an orange glow. I place them in the giant urn in the middle of the temple, just like Ah-ma did when we visited family in Taiwan. It makes me feel like she's here with me. I decide it's probably a good idea to say a little prayer, too. Maybe I'll ask Tin Hau to work a memory charm so everyone forgets about yesterday.

I go back home and hide in my bed with a book. At least I can imagine that I'm somewhere else, someone else. Rosie comes over in the afternoon and coaxes me out from under the comfort of my duvet.

"That was shocking. I can't believe she did that," Rosie says.

"I just don't understand why. I thought we were

friends," I say as Rosie pats my back gently. "I mean, after the hike, she was always around me, laughing at my jokes."

"And who else was always around?" asks Rosie, in a leading-question kind of tone.

"What do you mean? Just the usuals. Oh…and Theo." I flop back on my bed.

"Exactly. I think she's jealous. She definitely has a crush on him."

"But we're just friends," I say. Even though his dimples give me butterflies.

"Well, after you left last night, I saw Theo and her arguing."

"Really?" I sit up straight.

"Yes. None of us thought it was funny. Her mom was mad, too—she said it was a joke in bad taste and that it ruined the whole presentation."

I smile for the first time in hours, and I feel like the dark cloud hanging over my head is disappearing.

For homeroom on Monday morning, we get a preview of the new Tsien Wing arts center. In the lobby is a larger-than-life frame with a black silk cloth draped over it, waiting to be unveiled.

All the Grade 7 students file into the theater and take their seats in comfy dark red leather chairs. We start fiddling with the buttons on the armrest, making the seats recline up and down and the footrests go in and out as if we had our very own luxury La-Z-Boys. Mr. Gregg steps onstage and clears his throat into the microphone, waiting for us to settle down. After some futile attempts, he finally yells, "Stop it!" I put my chair back to its normal position and sit on my hands to prevent myself from sneaking another push at the buttons.

"Good morning, students. How fortunate we are to have such a generous family as the Tsiens at Tai Tam Prep. Their vision for the school is unsurpassed—"

I look over to Rosie in the row behind, and we lock eyes. I bite my lip to stifle a giggle at the praise Mr. Gregg is heaping on Gemma's family.

"—and we cannot even begin to show the depths of our gratitude." Mr. Gregg drones on. It's so over-the-top, and I can't believe Gemma's not shrinking in her chair. Instead, she smiles proudly and soaks up the praise like a sponge.

"And on to the challenge for you," he says. "This is a landmark event in a landmark year. And as you know, your grade will have the honor of headlining the wing's opening ceremony. It is very important that you make a good impression. Our reputation…" he pauses for effect "…is in your hands."

Rosie looks over at me and smiles. I smile back, but there's a niggle in my head about what Mr. Gregg just said about reputation. In our hands. Ours to drop and break.

"The descendants of the school's founder will be in attendance, as well as the Tsien family, of course—" he points at Gemma in the front row, and she stands and takes a bow "—as well as the head of a family who gave a very generous donation but wishes to remain anonymous." A ripple of murmurs spreads, and I follow Mr. Gregg's eyes. They land near Theo. At this, Theo looks down, as if something on the ground has suddenly caught his attention.

"I'm sure you will do the school proud," he says, concluding his speech. We give him a round of applause, and he steps off the stage, after doing his trademark mop of the head with a kerchief, and hands the microphone to Ms. Salonga, head of the Performing Arts department.

"Congratulations to you all. This will be such a memorable project for you to work on. Probably one of the highlights of your Tai Tam Prep careers." She adjusts her cat-eye glasses and tucks a lock of her chic black bobbed hair behind her ear. "You will be put in groups of six with students from your house, and you can choose to do a small performance on stage on the night or a visual project that will be exhibited in the auditorium lobby. We have four weeks until the curtain goes up, so you will need to work intensively. Your schedule has been modified so last period will be allotted to working on this. So, I encourage you to stay after school if needed, as this is a big opportunity to show off your work and our school to the community."

After a brief question-and-answer period, we get dismissed for break. I run and catch up with Rosie, and we link arms as we head back to our side of campus.

"Oh, my, this sounds rather daunting," Rosie says.

"And only four weeks to get it sorted," I say. I need to make last Friday night's fiasco up to my mom. I heard Dad tell her it wasn't my fault. She said she wasn't mad at me, and she even asked me if I was okay, but I can't shake the image of the disappointment on her face as the other parents laughed.

"And it looks like we'll be staying late after school for this," Rosie says.

"Oh, no. I was hoping to start playing some field hockey before team tryouts next month." Especially since I had to miss the last month of field hockey camp back in Toronto when we moved here.

I convince Rosie to grab a snack before next period starts. Food is always comforting. Rosie goes straight to the fruit bar, but I follow my nose to the bakery counter to find out what is responsible for that sweet smell permeating the cafeteria. It's a pineapple bun—bolo bao, the canteen lady tells me. It's on my list of snacks to try in Hong Kong. We sit down at a table, and I take a bite of the golden-hued baked delight. My teeth first bite through a crispy sweet top crust before reaching the pillow-like softness of the bun itself. It's delicious, but I'm a bit confused.

"I think they forgot to put the pineapple filling inside," I say.

Rosie giggles, "There's no pineapple in it. They call it a pineapple bun because the crackled sugar crust just makes it look like a pineapple."

"Oh." I shrug. "It's delicious anyway."

"They have ones with barbecued pork inside. So good. I'll take you to my favorite bakery to try it."

The day flies by, and I almost forget about the opening ceremony project until Ms. Salonga pops into French class and pulls me, Gemma, and Theo out and tells us we'll be in the same group. I hear Gemma give a little whimper. I've managed to avoid talking to her all day, and now I find out we'll be working together for a month. This is an added layer of stress I don't need.

We head to a room down the hall to meet the rest of our group. Inside, Rainbow, Snowy, and Rhys are sitting and waiting. It seems rather a big coincidence that Gemma is working with her two best friends, her obvious crush, Theo, and her eager sidekick, Rhys. But clearly, she didn't expect me to be in the group, too.

"Welcome to your first Earth House project, Holly-Mei." Rhys gives me a playful punch in the arm.

"Oh, goody," I say.

Ms. Salonga sits down and talks animatedly about the project, what resources are available to us, and her expectations. She seems more interested in letting students "have a chance to shine and do something they're passionate about" rather than using the event to boost Mr. Gregg's ego. The little knot in my stomach that I didn't even know was there slowly loosens, and I start to relax. Even though this is a big deal, it sounds like there will be lots of support, so we don't face-plant onstage. "Proposals in by next Monday before start of school, please," she says as she gets up and walks toward a different group of students.

Everyone in the group, except for me and Theo, starts talking excitedly about the ceremony and throwing around ideas.

"Let's do a robotics demonstration to show off the new innovation lab," Rhys says.

"Let's film a travel show where the destination is Tai Tam Prep. I can be the host since I have on-camera experience," Snowy says. "And I can upload it on my YouTube channel later."

"I'd rather do something that helps the environment. What about a beach cleanup on the school beach?" Rainbow asks.

"The school staff and the Environment Club do that every weekend," Gemma says.

"That gunk comes in from the Pearl River Delta every tide, no matter how often we clean it." Snowy sticks her tongue out and makes a grossed-out face.

"I know, but then we can use the materials we find to build a sculpture," Rainbow says.

"You want to build a sculpture out of rubbish?" Gemma asks, aghast. Rainbow looks slightly deflated.

Rubbish is what Dad calls *garbage*. "That sounds kind of cool," I say, imagining a tower of plastic bottles and tetra packs. Rainbow gives me a wide grin.

Theo finally pipes up with an idea. "If we really want to do something meaningful, why don't we actually go deeper into the community and help, like with a book-donation drive and storytelling session, or cooking and serving at a food kitchen in Sham Shui Po?" He continues on passionately, "We could encourage others to join us and then make a photo montage of it for display in the lobby."

I look at Theo, a little surprised but completely impressed at his suggestion.

"That would be so great," Snowy says. "My po po—" she turns to me as if to explain "—my mom's mom, lives in Sham Shui Po, and we help out at the community center every Sunday."

This is an interesting side to Snowy. I want to know more.

Gemma has other ideas, though. "Theo, that is a

heartfelt idea—" she puts her hand on her heart for extra effect "—and, of course, all of your ideas are good," she says as she looks at the rest of us. I brace myself for the *but* that will inevitably follow. "But I think you underestimate the importance of this event. Everyone will be watching. All eyes will be on us, and we have to make a big impression. There is no way that we are not getting up onstage and blowing them away with something spectacular."

I groan inwardly, but apparently not inwardly enough, because Gemma turns to me and says, "What about you, Holly-Mei? I suppose you think you have a better idea?" She raises her eyebrows in challenge.

"Maybe we should surreptitiously film people doing embarrassing things and make a montage of it. That's more your style, isn't it, Gemma?" I say. The others go silent, and Gemma bites her lip as I continue. "I am done with performing. I'd rather do the beach cleanup or community service. At least they raise awareness for a cause."

"No, Holly-Mei, we're doing a performance. We *need* to do a performance. My mother is a famous actress, and my father likes everything big and flashy. I mean, you've seen my house. I can't just be some sort of wallflower in the lobby."

"But—" I start to say, looking at the others in the group, but they don't meet my eyes, not even Theo.

"No *buts*. You're overruled. Maybe the expectations are lower where you come from, but the pressure to shine can't get any higher. We're. Doing. A. Performance." She enunciates the last few words slowly just in case I. Don't. Catch. Her. Meaning.

"Who made you boss?" I ask. Gemma's face turns a shade of pink, and her eyes take on a glassy sheen. Is she upset? Like, not angry-upset, but sad-upset?

"You still don't get it. My family's name is on the auditorium, and that means my family's name is on the line. Why do you think they chose the Grade 7s to lead the ceremony? Because of me. So I get to choose." She is so stubborn I don't think I could talk her down from her idea, even if I dared to try.

The ringing over the intercom lets us know that school is dismissed. Saved by the bell. I get up and start walking to the door.

"Where are you going?" Gemma asks, sounding genuinely surprised.

"I'm going to the hockey pitch to hit some balls." It's not a question, but it comes out of my mouth sounding like one, especially since everyone else is still sitting, note-pads in hand.

"Oh, no. We're not leaving until we have some decent ideas of what to perform. I'll ask my driver to do a run to Stanley and get us an order of bubble tea."

I sit back down, arms crossed, resigned.

After ninety minutes of brainstorming with nothing to show for it, we are finally dismissed by a stressed-out Gemma. As we race out of the classroom to catch the late bus, Snowy and Rainbow follow and point to a stairwell to the side of the lockers. I reluctantly step inside, thinking that they are going to gang up on me and yell at me for standing up to Gemma. Instead, Rainbow exhales before gently saying, "We get that you're frustrated. That Gemma is frustrating."

"She means well. She's not trying to be bossy just for the sake of being bossy," Snowy says.

"She honestly feels that pressure she's talking about. The pressure to look good in front of all those important people in order for her family to look good," says Rainbow.

"What? Like, look good in front of others to give her family face?" I ask.

"Something like that," Snowy says.

Ah-ma had explained the notion of *face* to me before. I still don't fully get it, but it's something about honor, respectability, and how people see you. And I'm afraid after last week at Gemma's, I might have cost my mom some face in front of Hong Kong's elite.

"So if we don't look good in front of the audience, we'll make our families look bad? And lose face?" I ask, hoping they will laugh and dismiss this ridiculous idea.

Instead, they say in unison, "Exactly."

I let that new way of looking at things spin in my head. If I look good, my mom will look good, and maybe it will help her with her job. But if I don't look good, my mom won't look good, and I might hinder her career. Slowly, something that feels like a concrete-filled balloon lands on me, pushing down until it settles like a weight on my shoulders.

Now that we've decided to perform onstage, we spend the rest of the week debating what exactly we'll do. Rainbow suggests a dance number about the different folk groups first living in Hong Kong, like the Hakka and Punti. Snowy suggests doing a lip sync to a mash-up of classic Cantopop music. I panic at the thought of singing in front of a theater full of people, even if it's pretend singing, and luckily Rhys shuts the idea down and instead suggests a skit about Bruce Lee.

"We can all wear those yellow jumpsuits and have 'Kung Fu Fighting' playing in the background." Rhys jumps up and does some martial arts moves with his hands. "Karate chop," he says as he pretends to chop the desk in half.

"Um, Rhys, karate is Japanese, obviously," Snowy says, with an audible exhale.

"What about a look back at the Hong Kong film history, featuring my mom?" Gemma suggests.

"That's a great idea," I say. Judging by Gemma's gaping mouth, she is pleasantly surprised. "I'll draft a proposal and send it to Ms. Salonga by Monday morning." I volunteer, not because I'm excited about this particular topic, but because I want to get a move on, so we can plan something that will not only make Gemma shine but my mom, too.

11

Up close, the water is the color of dark green jade. The four of us have come to the beach for a Saturday morning swim. Dad suggests making it a new weekly ritual. Mom and I tell him it sounds like a fun idea, but Millie says she'd rather watch cartoons. It's already hot, even though it's only eight o'clock, and the water is fresh and cool. Little fish swim around my toes but scatter as soon as I move my feet. I walk until the water comes up to my thighs, and then I plunge in and swim toward a pontoon. There are barely any waves, but I'm a little nervous as it's my first time swimming in the ocean so far out where my feet don't touch the bottom. I can't see past my hands, and I get a splash of water in my mouth, which is disgustingly salty and leaves my tongue feeling like I just licked a carpet. From the pontoon, I get an amazing view of Lofty Heights and decide that I'm pretty lucky to have the ocean as my playground.

When we arrive back home, Joy has a stack of golden French toast and freshly squeezed orange juice waiting for us.

"Thank you! I'm so hungry from swimming." I grab a banana and offer slices to everyone at the table.

After a few minutes of silence, except for the occasional "Yummy" or "These hit the spot," Dad starts speaking. "My research interview for my book was canceled today. What are you girls up to?"

"I'm going over to Lizzie's place soon. We're going to practice making soufflés." Millie has become fast friends with Henry's little sister.

"Sounds impressive," Mom says. "I've got to shower and head to my conference now. But I'll be back by six o'clock." She gets up from the table and gives Dad a quick peck on the cheek.

"And you, poppet?" Dad turns to me.

"I'm meeting Rosie in Causeway Bay this afternoon after her ballet class."

"Oh, I see," he says, sounding a touch disappointed. "Maybe I'll go out birding on the trails. The other day I spotted a red-whiskered bulbul."

"Well, I don't need to leave until two o'clock, so we can hang out together." As soon as I say this, Dad perks up and starts throwing suggestions of what we could be doing like go on a hike (too hot) or watch a documentary (too early). We settle on making some dumplings that Joy can fry up later for dinner.

Dad and I pop to the shop downstairs for the ingredients. We cheat a bit and buy ready-made dumpling wrappers because we're not sure we can make them properly without Ah-ma. Back in the kitchen, Dad pulls out a wooden cutting board and the biggest knife he can find and starts gently peeling the ginger. No need to worry about counting his fingers like I do with Ah-ma because he chops as if he's in slow motion, almost like he doesn't want to hurt the ginger.

"So tell me about this big group project you're working on," Dad says.

"Well, it's sort of top secret. You'll find out at the gala thing when we get onstage."

"Sounds intriguing." Dad flashes me a grin.

"I hope so, although right now, it's all about Gemma and her family." I rinse the prawns in the colander and pat them with a paper towel.

"Well, I'm sure all the other group members have interesting tidbits in their family histories."

Dad looks up from chopping the prawns and wipes his forehead with his arm. He points at my bamboo shoots and tells me to keep chopping while he mixes the ginger, prawns, and minced pork in a bowl.

"That's true. I know Theo's family has been here for generations. Snowy said her great-grandfather biked over from China after the war."

I throw my bamboo shoots in Dad's mixing bowl, and I reach for the dumpling wrappers.

"And it can be about recent arrivals, too. All newcomers contribute something worthwhile to the fabric of society," he says.

"Rainbow said her mother started an environment charity last year." I scoop one spoonful of the filling into the middle of the round white wrapper and fold it, but it doesn't stick like Ah-ma's handmade wrappers do. "What about us?"

Dad looks at me and gives a smile. "We just got here,

but I'm sure we'll find some way to give back and get involved."

I nod along to his words of wisdom. When this project is over, I'm going to convince Millie to join one of the community-service clubs at school with me.

He watches me struggle to fold a few dumplings before saying, "Don't tell your Ah-ma, but look what I found." Out of the drawer, he pulls out a white plastic circle with a handle on each side. "A dumpling press. Isn't it genius?" He places the wrapper in the middle, adds the filling, and folds one side onto the other. "Voilà," he says. "Perfect dumplings."

They look sort of like pierogies and nothing like the dainty folded dumplings Ah-ma makes, but I'm sure they'll still taste great. When we're finished making them all, I take a selfie of us with our tray of dumplings and send it to Ah-ma.

I wash my hands and run to my room, almost slipping on the sleek polished teak floors. I whip open my laptop and start typing a draft of our group's proposal. Instead of just focusing on Gemma's family, I decide we are going to do something about all our families. When I'm done, I think for a second about putting this new topic on the chat to check with the group, but I'm sure they'll be fine with it. Besides, I'm tired of being bossed around by Gemma. She still hasn't even apologized to me about the video.

Ah-Lok drops me off at the MTR station. He said he could bring me all the way to Causeway Bay, but I want to be independent and take the subway on my own. The platform at the Ocean Park station is aboveground, clean, and full of sunlight. And I only need to go three stops to my destination with one change. I jump on the train, and the bell trills to signal the doors are closing. A giant, boldly colored ad for whitening cream above a row of seats catches my eye. A doll-like model, who looks almost too delicate and beautiful to be real, holds a bright blue jar in her manicured hand. A speech bubble next to her says *Reveal your true inner beauty.* I touch my ponytail and subconsciously look toward the doors, hoping no one will notice my tan or lack of makeup. But, when I dare to look around, I notice the girls and women on the train are of a whole variety of skin tones, from light and bright to rich and dark. And all equally beautiful. I guess real-life is a multitude of gorgeous colors.

Rosie waves to me at the station exit, her blond hair in a tight ballet bun, and her pink knapsack over her shoulder.

"I'm famished. Fancy a snack?" she asks.

"For sure. Bubble tea?"

"My ballet teacher is trying to get us to cut down on that."

"What? That's crazy." I look at Rosie's tall, lean frame.

"I know, right?" She giggles. "But she didn't say anything about matcha ice cream. The place around the corner makes their own cones."

I can smell the sweet waffles before I step into the shop. We order two mixed cones, and a man takes one of the freshly made waffle cones out of a stack and pulls a lever for the soft-serve ice cream, and two ribbonlike stripes of vanilla and matcha green tea flow out. The vanilla part is light, not too sweet, and the green tea is richer and leaves a tiny trace of matcha powder on my tongue. Rosie takes me on a tour of the area as we lick our cones. On the various little streets, she points out her favorite places for ramen, sushi, and egg waffles. "There's where you get char siu bolo bao." She points to a corner bakery,

"We'll go next time." We also pass a few boutiques with cheap and cheerful clothes from Korea and Japan.

"That would look so cute on you." Rosie points to a denim jumpsuit with cap sleeves and a drawstring waist in the shop window. I make a mental note to ask Dad for money to do a little clothes shopping next time. He only gave me money for a new bathing suit, since mine is getting too small and was riding up this morning.

We push through the crowds at a huge department store called Sogo and go up the escalator to the seventh floor, marked *Sports*. I pick out a one-piece navy Speedo racer-back style with pink and silver stars across the front.

"That's cute. It's very you," Rosie says.

"Next time we come to Causeway Bay, I wouldn't mind getting some new clothes, so I don't always look like I'm going to the gym like my mom is always teasing."

"I have a couple of skirts and dresses that I'm too tall for. I can give them to you."

"Skirts and dresses." I laugh as I look down at my shorts and baggy T-shirt. Those will definitely make Mom happy. And maybe I can branch out my style. Plus I can wear them with my Birks or Converse.

We do a loop of Victoria Park and sit under the shade

of a tree to chill and chat. A group of elderly Chinese people do tai chi on the grass nearby. I smile at an old lady who looks a little like Ah-ma from this distance. She smiles back.

"What are you guys doing for the gala?" Rosie asks. "We're planning on doing a modern dance number. One of my groupmates' dad is a Cantopop star, and he's going to do a special recording for us. And the choreographer from his latest video will put together our routine."

"That's so exciting." Wow, they are going to have a knockout show. We definitely need to up our game.

"What about you guys?"

"We're still in the early stages, but something about all our families and how we contribute to Hong Kong."

"Oh, that will be interesting. But I'm surprised Gemma is happy to share the spotlight." Rosie giggles.

"Actually, she just wants to be onstage. So I'm sure she'll be fine with it."

"What? You haven't asked her?"

"Oh, it'll be fine. It's basically what we agreed, but I'm just tweaking it and making it better." And after hearing about Rosie's group, I'm so glad I am.

Rosie bites her lip but doesn't say anything.

* * *

Back home, Millie comes into my room without knocking, as usual, and dives onto my bed.

"How was the soufflé-making?" I ask, turning from my laptop.

"Fun, but hard. It took us two tries before we made ones that didn't collapse," Millie says. "How are things with you? I can't believe you have to work on your project with Gemma." She rolls on her stomach and rests her chin in her hands.

"Oh, that's old news." I shake my head as if I'm shaking off a pesky mosquito. "Everything's fine. She's being totally nice to me now. Bossy, but nice."

"Look, you don't need to be BFFs with everyone. We just got here. Take your time to meet people and make real friends. There's no rush."

"You sound like Ah-ma." I let out a big sigh.

"I talked to her this morning. She's was asking how we're settling in, and I told her about what happened." Millie puffs her cheeks.

"You told her? It's over now," I say, annoyed.

"She also asked me if you've reached out to Natalie," she says in a gentle tone.

"Why should I? I've got a new life now. Things are great, never better. Perfect."

By dinnertime on Sunday, I'm done polishing my final edit, and I send it to Ms. Salonga. I sit back in my chair pleased with myself. I've just written a knockout group proposal.

12

On Tuesday afternoon, Ms. Salonga meets with each group individually to go over the proposals. I can tell she's pleased with ours as she's smiling when she sits down at our table.

"Wonderful work, guys. I like how you acknowledged the various contributions of all your families. It's a statement on how we all contribute in our own way." She hands me the proposal with some comments and then gets up and moves to another group. I keep the paper facedown and bite my lip before I turn around to face the group. It's great that Ms. Salonga likes the proposal, but I never actually told the others that I changed it.

I take a deep breath and paste on a smile. "Great, proposal approved. I tweaked it a touch, by the way." I don't pause before continuing. "So I guess we dive in and write the script?"

"Let me see that." Gemma rips the proposal from my hand. "This is not what we discussed."

"It sort of is, but expanded. Just because it's not your idea doesn't mean it's no good."

"Why didn't you run it by us?" Theo asks calmly.

"And ask us if it was okay?" Rhys asks.

"But she loves it," I say. They still look at me, waiting for more of an explanation. "Look, we have to be amazing, don't we? We have to knock their socks off. Rosie's group is getting a professional choreographer. If we want to look good, make our parents look good, we need something more meaningful."

"I get it," Snowy says.

"Me, too, but you still should have run it by us," Rainbow says.

The group is a bit deflated, so we decide to go straight home when school lets out. Rosie stays late to work with her group, and Rhys and Theo sit at the back of the bus, so the seat next to me on the bus home is empty. I hope I haven't made a mess of things. Images of Natalie and my classmates back home flash through my head—how they whispered when I walked by, how they ignored me at recess, how I had to sneak my sandwich into the library so no one would see me eating by myself. One small mistake cost me all my friends. What if I've pushed everyone at my new school away already? I pull out my phone and check the group chat. No new messages, but I breathe a sigh of relief that I haven't been kicked off it. Yet.

I FaceTime with Ah-ma when I get home. She is an early riser and goes for a sunrise walk around the block to start her day. I catch her just as she is heading out.

"Baobei, what nice surprise. Are you okay?"

"Hai keyi," I say, *so so.* I lie down on my bed, snuggled safely between pillows and hold my phone in the air.

"Did something happen at school today?" she asks, as if reading my mind.

"I dunno," I say. "Maybe?"

From the look on her face on the screen, even though it's partially covered by her finger on the camera, I can tell she's waiting for me to expand.

"We have this group-project proposal. I changed what we agreed to do, but I was just trying to make it better."

"And what was consequence?" she asks gently.

Ah-ma, Mom, and Dad are always reminding me and Millie that our actions have consequences.

"Now everyone is mad at me." I look everywhere else on the screen but her face.

"Oh, baobei," she says. I feel an ache on my shoulder where I miss her touch.

"I thought I managed to skip the chi ku part." The bitterness. "How can I make the sweetness come faster?" I swallow hard to make the lump in my throat go away.

"Patience, my love. Your idea for project is good. But," she says tenderly, "you need to take other opinions into consideration. Everyone wants to feel their ideas valuable."

I sigh. I know she's right, but I'm just not sure what to do about it.

The next day in last period, Gemma announces that she's leaving right after school for a meeting in town.

"With that consultant?" Snowy asks.

"Yes, my mom is dragging me."

"What kind of consultant?" I ask.

Gemma turns to me and narrows her eyes. "You wouldn't understand."

She's clearly still annoyed at me. In fact, everyone is

a bit meh. Rhys sits there with his arms crossed, and Rainbow doodles in her notebook. Theo chews on the string of his hoodie.

"Look, guys," I start, "I should have asked before I changed the proposal. Everyone's ideas have value, not just mine. I'm sorry."

That seems to satisfy them. Gemma gives me a nod and a "Fine," and the others say, "It's okay." Theo gives me a smile, dimples and all.

For the next hour we work on hashing out a script.

Rhys talks about his dad, ex-air force turned airline pilot, who had the chance to fly a member of the royal family over from London. I talk about Mom working hard and getting the promotion to the first female COO of her Hong Kong–based company.

"What about you, Theo? Do you want to put in anything about the pirates?"

Gemma gasps loudly. There are several sets of open mouths.

Shoot. Did I just do that blurting thing Mom was talking about? I don't need another reason to alienate my friends.

Theo starts laughing. "I think those are just rumors.

My mother's family did build a shipping company when the British took over Hong Kong. But we can dress up as pirates onstage if you want."

Rainbow and Gemma burst out laughing. Rhys starts to regale us in the background with "Aargh" and "Ahoy, matey." Snowy chips in with a "Walk the plank, grrr!"

For the first time in ages, I'm free when the dismissal bell goes. Instead of hopping on the school bus, I run excitedly toward the field hockey pitch. There are a few people hitting balls into an open net. I grab a handful of bright orange balls and a stick from a wheelie bin, walk over to the D, the shooting circle, and ask if I can join in.

A boy in a white baseball cap looks up and smiles. "Sure," he says and moves to make room for me.

I take a few hits. Some miss completely, and some manage to barely make it in. I'm so rusty after just a few weeks of not playing. I watch in wonder as the boy next to me in the cap does some reverse stick-hits, which all hit the backboard with a bang. I put my head back down and swing at my ball, but I top it, so instead of sailing toward the net, it sails in his direction. I let out a whelp as it flies at his head. He ducks just in time, but not before it knocks off his baseball cap.

I run toward him. "I'm sooo sorry." I pick up the hat and hand it to him. "Really, I didn't mean to try and take your head off."

"No worries," he says with a little laugh. He pushes his thick floppy black hair out of his eyes before putting the cap back on. "You new here?"

I nod.

"I'm Devinder Singh. My friends call me Dev."

"Hey, nice to meet you, Dev. I'm Holly-Mei. I just started in Grade 7. 7A."

"I'm in 7B." He flashes a megawatt smile, and his face lights up.

"Then you're in Rosie's class. She's my cousin."

"Why haven't I seen you on the pitch before? Are you trying out for the team?" he asks.

"I'm definitely trying out. It's just that my group for this gala thingy is super keen, and we have to stay every day after school to work on it. I can't wait until all this stress is over." I crack another ball toward the net; this time it goes in. "What are you doing for the exhibition?"

"Our group is doing a photography exhibit about

the Indian community in Hong Kong. Some of our families have been here for generations. People don't realize there are lots of non-Chinese communities here. It'll be nice to show a different side of Hong Kong."

"Sounds super interesting."

"You guys?"

"Top secret," I say with a laugh. "Hey, can you teach me how to reverse stick-hit?"

"If you promise not to take my head off," he says, smiling. "Now, show me what you can do."

I take the ball and push it to my left. I flip my stick and bend down to hit it with the sweet spot just above the hook. But the ball trickles forward. "I can't get any power."

"You're raising your right leg. Keep both feet on the ground."

I try again, and this time I make strong contact with the ball. It goes way out, but at least it has good power. We hit balls and chat for the rest of the afternoon. It turns out that he plays for the Hong Kong U14 hockey team, which is so impressive. I end up missing the late bus, and I have to figure out how to take the public bus home by myself. But it was so much fun. Totally worth it.

***

The rest of the week passes in a blur as we do some research online and in the library. Things seem to be going well with the project, so I'm surprised that when I get home on Friday, Mom calls me into the dining room and tells me, "We need to discuss something," which is code for *You're in trouble.*

Mom's sitting at the table, lips pursed and hands folded over a piece of paper. She's still in her work suit, so she looks extra intimidating. I pause before sitting down, eyes searching the paper for a hint of what's to come. It's our group's proposal marked up by Ms. Salonga. Mom must have found it on my desk. I breathe in deeply and take a seat.

After a few seconds, Mom starts speaking. "I have heard all about your proposal. How you changed it without consulting with your group. That is not good group-work behavior."

"How did you find out?"

"People talk. Hong Kong is a big city, but a small one at the same time."

"That was ages ago. Everything is good now." At least I think it is. Mom is always telling me I need to learn to sort things out on my own, and now when I already have, she's getting involved. It's ridiculous that adults care what's happening at school.

"No parent wants to hear that their child has behaved badly." I can hear the disappointment in her voice.

I nod meekly and look down at my hands. "I'm sorry, Mom."

"Well, it's done. As long as you guys do well at the exhibition. Are you sure your group is equipped to succeed? I hear other groups are hiring professionals to help."

"We're not getting graded on it," I protest. I can't deal with her putting more pressure on me than I'm already putting on myself.

"But you are, in a way. We're all being judged. Remember, important people will be in the audience, and you have one shot to make a good impression."

"Is this that whole *face* thing again? What happened to *Try your best* or *A for effort*, like you used to tell us?"

"The rules in this world are a little different."

"Well, maybe it sucks to be in this world. Maybe we should go back to plain old Maple Grove Elementary so we don't need to deal with these stupid rules." I cross my arms in front of my chest and give my poutiest pout.

She lets out a loud sigh. "I don't have time for this discussion. I have a work dinner to get ready for." She gets up from the table and takes a step away before turning back toward me. "You know what? I don't think you're taking this project seriously enough." She taps the proposal with her finger. "How about this, then? If you don't do well at the exhibition, you won't be allowed to try out for the school field hockey team."

I can't believe her. I'm working so hard to make sure we look good. So she looks good. And she's planning on punishing me? This is so unfair. I get up from the table and head out the front door.

"Where do you think you're going?" she asks.

I ignore her, walk out the door, and press the Down button for the lift.

The beach is heaving with people. I expected it to be empty, but it's full of families having picnics and playing with paper lanterns. Laughter and chatter reach my ears. Kids squeal as they run to the water, sounding surprised and delighted every time they get splashed by the waves. I've been so busy thinking about this performance, that I totally forgot that it's Mid-Autumn Festival tonight. I guess

Mom forgot, too—another family tradition left behind, just like Friday-night movies. It's one of the biggest festivals in the Chinese calendar. It's supposed to be a time for families to come together and give thanks, like Thanksgiving, but it looks like we're not doing anything as a family tonight. I find a quiet area at the edge of the beach and sit down in the sand, still warm from the hot, sunny day, and look out onto the horizon, counting the passing cargo ships. As the sun sets, I lie back and stare at the sky and try and make out the shadow of the goddess Chang'e on the full, glowing moon. She's supposed to grant wishes, but I don't know what I should wish for. To rewind the clock and hand in a different proposal? For our performance to be a success? Or maybe to be able to pack up and go back home, away from these new rules that I don't understand.

The sand crunches next to me as someone walks up.

"I figured you might be here." Dad sits down beside me.

I sit up and shake the sand from my hair.

"Are you all right, poppet?" Dad asks.

"Yes and no," I say.

He gives me a hug. I can't help it: I start to cry into his shoulder.

"Maybe this weekend we can bake some mooncakes together as a family. I can ask Ah-ma for her recipe," he says gently.

I pop my head up and wipe my nose on the back of my hand. "I would love that. Thanks."

He puts his arm around me, and we sit in silence, admiring Chang'e, the lady and spirit in the moon.

13

Theo claims he has a brilliant idea for our project, but he's not going to reveal it until we do a team field trip this weekend. He says it'll be *good for our group's morale*, as if he were our teacher. Plus, he promised to buy us lunch. I'm excited about the dim sum, so I go without complaint.

Uncle Charlie drops me and Rhys off in the city center where we meet the others. We walk over to the Peak Tram station and line up to ride the famous funicular that goes up to Victoria Peak. The station is like a minimuseum displaying life-size photos of the original tram and its riders from the 1800s. I close my eyes and imagine women dripping with sweat in their heavy petticoats and holding parasols to block out the blazing sun as they jostle their way to the seats. The tram ride is short and bumpy, and the incline is almost forty-five degrees, so our backs are pushed back against the chairs, making it hard to turn around and talk to each other. Although the tram car itself is old-fashioned, we get off in a modern but tacky shopping mall, complete with a Burger King and celebrity wax museum, putting an end to my historical daydreams.

"Let's do the circular trail. You'll be able to see the old mansions," Theo says to the group.

"You'll also get to see all sides of Hong Kong Island," Rainbow says to me.

"Sounds perfect." I walk briskly toward the exit, eager to get out of the freezing air-conditioning and into the fresh air.

The air is cooler on the Peak, which, Gemma explains, is why the taipans, the heads of foreign businesses in early colonial days, all had houses up here. We walk along a paved path and weave around a few tourists and people out for exercise, passing old historic stucco houses, some in pastel colors, some still in use, and some abandoned, overrun with mold and moss.

Looking down on the northwest side, we get a bird's-eye view of the harbor, and I can trace the road back over the suspension bridge to the airport. The streets are full of cars, and the water full of cargo ships, but from so high up, everything looks peaceful, and the only sound is of the leaves rustling.

Theo stops and points straight ahead. "Here, look." The view cuts across the western part of Hong Kong all the way to Lantau Island.

"Oooh, I can see Disneyland." Snowy points toward some structures at the base of green hills across the way. "That pointy thing is the Princess Castle."

"And that white triangle is Space Mountain," Rhys says. "Let's make a day of it once we're done this project."

We all get excited and declare how fun that sounds. Except Theo.

"Guys, I didn't bring you here to talk about Mickey Mouse. I brought you to see the house." Theo points to a small white house hidden behind lush forest canopy. He leads us down an unmarked trail and stops in front of an ornate but rusted iron gate and then pulls a key out of his backpack.

"Wow, that looks so old," I say. It looks like one of those antique skeleton keys that opens secret doors.

He puts the key into the lock. After a loud click, it

swings open with a high-pitched creaking sound. As Theo walks forward, the rest of us glance at each other before following him down a cobblestone path, our phone lights shining, trying not to trip over the tangle of tree roots on the ground.

"Where *are* we?" Rainbow asks in wonder.

"You'll see," Theo says.

"Are there any snakes here?" Gemma asks.

"Don't worry, stay beside me, and I'll protect you." Rhys puts his arm out, and Gemma takes it. I feel my eyes roll back inside my head.

We stop in a clearing that looks like an old courtyard: a stone table and bench to one side, and a small pagoda to the other.

"This is Lofty Gardens, or what's left of it. My great-great-grandfather had it built as a gift for his new bride," Theo says. "I thought we could tell their story for my section of the performance. I had to get permission from my parents first, but they said okay."

"Oh, I've heard of this place. I didn't know it really existed." Snowy tries to peer through a window, but green fuzzy mold has rendered it opaque.

I wonder if Dad would have come across this place in his research for his novel.

"What's their story?" I ask, intrigued.

"My great-great-grandfather, Lo Xian Dao, was from Shanghai, and he moved to Hong Kong after studying in London. He met a high-ranking Scottish merchant's daughter, Ailsa Fitzwilliam, and they fell in love."

"How romantic," Gemma says with a sigh.

"Well, it wasn't that simple. People on both sides thought there shouldn't be mixing." Theo looks directly at me, I guess because we're the only two mixes in the group.

I nod, encouraging him to continue, trying to ignore the dull ache in my heart I suddenly feel for people that I've never met who lived years before my time.

"But they got married anyway and lived happily in this house for a few years."

"Ailsa Fitzwilliam, like, as in your last name, Fitzwilliam-Lo?" I ask, scratching my head.

"Yes, the families first came together almost one hundred years ago. Then broke apart until my parents got together."

"Broke apart?" Rainbow asks.

"Just after they had a baby, my great-grandfather George Dao Lo, the civil war in China started. Xian Dao felt it was his duty to return to fight against the Communists. He never returned. Ailsa was heartbroken, and she died shortly after from dengue fever."

"That is the saddest thing I've ever heard." Snowy blows her nose into a Hello Kitty tissue.

"What happened to the baby?" Rainbow asks.

"The baby was raised by his father's brother and his wife as one of their own. But they couldn't bear to live in this house, and it's been empty ever since."

"What a tragic love story. This will move people and make their hearts melt. *It's perfect.*" Gemma claps her hands together. "We should end with this. Let's do it chronologically backward, from newest story—" she points at me "—and ending with the oldest one."

No one dares to challenge her. I think we're all just relieved Gemma is finally happy with an idea.

"I'll play Ailsa," she announces. "And of course, Theo, you'll play your great-great-grandfather."

The leafy switchback trail from the Peak into Central is so steep that my legs are like jelly. If I had known we were going to walk all the way down, I would have worn proper running shoes and shorts. Instead, I'm dressed in a new hand-me-down cotton dress from Rosie. Thankfully, I'm wearing Converse instead of strappy sandals like Snowy. We've already had to stop so she could put on a couple of Band-Aids. Luckily, I always carry an assortment of first-aid things wherever I go.

By the time we arrive at City Hall for dim sum, we're ravenous. The nondescript gray boxy building is striking because it is so different to the flashy high-rises around it. Inside, the carpet is the color of grape juice, and the walls are plastered with bright posters of upcoming events: chamber music, Chinese orchestra, Cantonese opera. We race up to the restaurant on the second floor. Theo grabs a number from the electronic ticket-dispensing machine, and while the others wait in the lobby, I peek inside. It's a huge room with ornate golden chandeliers and red velvet chairs, and it looks ready for a wedding, but it's full of casual lunchtime activity. After a few minutes, we get seated by the window, facing the ferry piers and a Ferris wheel.

"This is my favorite dim sum place. I just love the trolley dollies." Rhys points to the waitresses pushing carts filled with food around the room, yelling out the names of their dim sum goodies. People in turn yell their orders back at them. Our table is soon filled with little baskets of steaming har gau shrimp dumplings and fluffy sweet pork char siu bao buns. We load our table with porcelain plates of cheung fan—rice rolls filled with shrimp—and various bamboo baskets of delicious dishes. I use my newly learned mm goi with the servers—the magic word that means *excuse me, please*, and *thank you*. After we're done with savory stuff, we wait for the dessert cart to come around with some dan tat—egg custard tarts. My heart jumps when I see a sign for tang yuan—peanut dumplings in a sweet ginger broth. I wave to the lady, and she places a bowl on our table and stamps our card. This is my favorite dessert. I've only ever seen the peanut dumplings at Ping's Palace, our regular dim sum place back in Toronto. In other places, they are usually filled with black sesame, which is also good, but it's not the same. Ah-ma makes peanut tang yuan for me every year on my birthday, so it's doubly special finding it here. I devour the dumplings and let the sweet and salty mix of the peanuts and sugared ginger rest in my mouth a few seconds before I wash it down with tea.

"Theo, where to next?" Rhys asks.

"The history museum," Theo says.

"Museum?" Rhys lets out a little whinge.

"There's a special exhibit on with some old photos."

"It'll be good research. I can get some ideas for set design," Rainbow says.

"And I can get some ideas for the costumes," Gemma says.

"We're not walking anymore, are we?" Snowy asks.

"Don't worry, I have more Band-Aids," I say.

Across the footbridge from City Hall is the Star Ferry pier, where we'll catch a boat across the harbor to Tsim Sha Tsui, otherwise known as TST.

"The best view of the skyline is from the other side," Rainbow says.

The green-and-white-painted ferry looks like it hasn't changed in a century. We sit in a row of simple white wooden seats decorated with punched-out holes in a star motif. The floor and reversible seat backs are made of shiny dark wood that reminds me of our antique English dresser. A man in a navy sailor's uniform pulls the gangplank closed with a cord, and another sailor throws a thick rope off the pier onto the deck. The sides of the ferry are open, and I'm sitting closest to the side, so I get lightly splashed as we move through the choppy water. My stomach tightens as we go up and down, but I'm soothed by the wind on my face. I close my eyes and take a deep breath through my nose, but instead of fresh salty air, I get a whiff of diesel fumes. My stomach tightens further, and I feel my lunch start to creep up toward my throat.

"Holly-Mei, are you okay? You look a little green," Theo says.

I don't say anything, but make a wave motion with my hand.

"Give me your arms," he says.

I do as he says without opening my eyes. He presses the insides of my wrists.

"Acupressure. My maa maa used to do this when I got seasick."

I exhale and relax for the first time since setting foot on the ferry. I look around and take in the view. To my right, I see the buildings of TST getting closer. To my left, I see Gemma eyeing Theo's hands on my wrists. She gives me a cold stare, then she rearranges her face into a smirk. The same smirk I saw when she made fun of me for never having been to Paris. I brace myself for what's coming.

"Holly-Mei, since you're new, I'd be happy to give you

recommendations for all the best salons." Gemma has a sweet smile plastered on her face.

"Thanks. I probably need a haircut," I say.

"My manicure place is cheap and cheerful," she says as she eyes my unpainted nails before glancing at her perfectly painted fingernails. "And I have a great place for threading—you know, for your eyebrows. Poor thing, you mustn't have had yours done since you moved here."

I reflexively raise my hands and touch my eyebrows, which causes Theo to lose his grip on my wrists. Gemma flashes me another smirk, which I take as her having achieved her goal, whatever that may be.

We dock on the other side of the harbor with a light thud. The sailor inside throws the rope to someone on shore who wraps it around a short, thick pole. The gangplank lowers, and we follow the crowd out.

"How's your stomach?" Theo asks.

"Not bad. Thanks so much for your help," I say.

Snowy comes running up. "After the museum, I'm going to pop into Harbour City mall to look for a new bikini for your party next Saturday," Snowy says to Gemma.

"Great idea. I'll join you. I need a new beach cover," Rainbow says as she puts her sunglasses on. "I hope my allowance will cover it."

Gemma turns to Theo. "You're still coming, right?"

"I wouldn't miss it, Gems." Theo turns to me and says, "You'll have to try the slide. It's faster than a roller coaster." He makes a whooshing motion with his arm.

"Slide?" I ask. I look at Gemma, and her face looks like she just bit into a lemon wedge.

"Yes, on my family boat for my birthday party." She hesitates and looks over at Theo before saying to me, "You can come, too, if you want."

Except for the occasional canoe and today's Star Ferry, I've never been on a real boat before, so I jump at the chance. "Sure, I'd love to." Plus, I know her invitation is reluctant, and it's fun watching her squirm.

"Fantastic," says Theo. "It's gonna be so much fun."

The six of us each get a cone from the Mister Softee truck by the edge of the boardwalk. None of us are actually hungry after our dim sum feast, but no one can resist ice cream. And the thought of having something cold in the September heat is too appealing. The icy sweetness dissolves on my tongue and perks me up. Rainbow is right. The view from this side of the harbor is picture-postcard perfect. We walk along the boardwalk called the Avenue of Stars and pass a statue of Bruce Lee and try our handprints over those of Michelle Yeoh, Jet Li, and a cartoon pig named McDull.

Snowy pops the remains of her cone in her mouth and says, "Come close, it's selfie time." She puts her arms around me and Rainbow, and says, "One, two, three, cheese!" Both of them have their fingers in V-formation.

"Why do you have your fingers like that? In the V?" I ask.

They look at each other, shrug, and giggle.

"I don't know, to be honest," Rainbow says. "Something I picked up after moving here."

"It's just automatic," Snowy says. She plays with some filters on the photo and shows us the result. I look like an anime character with giant saucer eyes and sparkles in my hair. "You're Insta famous now," she announces.

The Hong Kong Museum of History starts out with the city's story from the beginning of time, like geological formations and prehistoric people. We speed through that part until we reach a huge room filled with vintage costumes, folk instruments, and bygone-era furniture. I love watching history documentaries with Dad, so seeing all this old stuff brings it to life. There's even a replica junk—

those old teak boats with red sails you see on postcards. I wonder if Gemma's boat will look like this.

I walk into the replica Hakka farmhouse, and Gemma is there on her own. I turn to go, but she says, "I didn't mean to make fun of your eyebrows. I was just annoyed, you know?"

"It's fine, whatever."

"I'm just protective of Theo."

"Why, do you have a *crush* on him?" I ask, part accusation, part interrogation.

She reddens, and I feel good getting her back for embarrassing me on the ferry. Before she can respond, Rhys walks in and tells us the rest of the group is moving upstairs to the special photo exhibition.

We push back a thick velvet curtain and step back in time as we enter the exhibit, Prominent Families of Early Twentieth-Century Hong Kong. Black-and-white photos of couples and families fill the room, both British and Chinese. Some Chinese men are in traditional dress, a few even have a long ponytail called the queue. Others are in Western-style suits. Most of the Chinese women are in cheongsams with short capped sleeves and silk-rope knotted buttons. There are some of these traditional dresses on display, and Gemma coos over the detailing and embroidery.

"I wish we could try these on," Rainbow says.

"Oh, they're much too fragile. But I can see if I can get something similar made for us for the performance," Gemma says. "Of course, they won't be as elaborate, but the audience won't be able to tell."

Theo is stopped in front of an enlarged photo of a mixed couple, a handsome Chinese man in a tuxedo and a beautiful light-haired woman in a satin scoop-neck ball gown.

"Is this them?" I ask.

He nods. "I've never looked this closely at their photo before."

We gather around him and gaze in silence at this window into the past. A photo of Xian Dao and Ailsa Lo, Theo's great-great-grandparents.

"They look so in love," Snowy says dreamily.

"What a beautiful necklace," Rainbow says of the jade necklace in the photo.

"It looks like it weighs a ton," I say.

"Hey, is this the real thing?" Rhys asks, pointing to a glass box under a spotlight where a jade necklace is on display. It looks like a pearl necklace, but all the beads are vivid green and carved in delicate patterns of birds and flowers, with a large jade pendant rimmed in bright yellow gold.

"It was his wedding present to her. He had a thistle carved on the pendant as a nod to her Scottish home."

"It's exquisite," Gemma says. "Look at the details in the carvings."

The rest of us move on, and Snowy takes some photos of the exhibition pieces for our research, but Gemma stays planted in front of the necklace. After half an hour, we start to leave, but she doesn't budge.

"Gemma, are you coming? I think we have everything we need," Rainbow says.

"Not everything," she says.

"What do you mean?" Snowy asks.

"I need this." She points to the necklace. "If I wear this on stage, we'll definitely be a success."

"Funny, Gemma." Rainbow tries to pull her friend along, but Gemma stands firm.

"I mean it." Gemma doubles down and stamps her foot like a toddler. I want to tell her she's being ridiculous. That necklace won't make or break our performance. But I remember how much she feels is at stake for her—like she's under as much pressure as I am. Instead of blurting out what is spinning around in my head, I try and see things as she might see them and say what she might want to hear. I touch her gently on the arm and say, "It's a good idea. It really is."

She nods as I speak. I continue. "Maybe your mother has something like it in her jewelry box you can borrow. Or maybe we can find some green glass beads and make something similar. Like you said before, the audience won't be able to tell."

"Hmm, maybe you're right," she says softly, resigned. She follows my lead out of the room, never taking her eyes off the jade treasure.

14

The next Saturday, on a cloudless sunny morning, I get ready for Gemma's twelfth-birthday party on her family boat. In the kitchen, I put some freshly baked brownies in a container in case I get hungry.

"I hope I don't throw these up," I say, snapping the lid shut.

"Do you get seasick? I'll make you some ginger tea. It'll help calm your stomach," Joy says.

"Really?" The tension in my tummy relaxes a touch.

"I don't like boats, either. My mother used to make fresh ginger tea for me whenever we had to go on a ferry."

I help cut the ginger, and we put it in a pot of boiling water before pouring it into my thermos. "Thanks, Joy."

Millie pops into the kitchen and shoves a brownie in her mouth. "I want to go, too. It's the party everyone at school is talking about. Even Lizzie is going."

I leave Millie to console herself with more brownies. I can't help it if Gemma invited Henry's little sister.

I reach Rosie's place, and she answers the door, her voice full of sunshine.

"Good morning!" She's wearing a sky-blue sundress and bright pink sunglasses on her head.

"Do you have your hat?" She eyes my beach bag.

"I brought two, in case one blows away in the wind. Are we supposed to bring anything? Can we stop at the shop downstairs for some juice or soda pop?"

"The boat is fully catered, so there will be plenty of stuff," Rhys says as he tries to squeeze a rugby ball into his already overflowing backpack.

"Gemma's parents will be there, right? Mom and Dad were asking," I say.

"I'm sure they will be," says Rosie reassuringly.

When we get to the lobby of the marina club, there are already at least fifty other people gathered for the birthday party. Dev Singh walks in and flashes me his bright smile. I instinctively touch my ponytail as I give him a *hello* wave back. He comes over and greets me, Rosie, and Rhys. I notice that although he and Theo give each other a nod, neither smiles.

Gemma emerges from the middle of the group to stand on top of something and yells, "Who's ready for my birthday?" to a chorus of cheers. "Then, follow me!" She leads us down the walkway to her waiting boat.

My jaw almost drops to the floor. Her boat is a huge, sleek yacht with so many floors it needs its own elevator. It looks like I've been transported to a photo shoot for one of those travel magazines you see at the doctor's office. The wood floors are so polished I can see my reflection, and the blankets on the outdoor sofas are so soft I want to curl up and have a nap. Gemma gives us a tour of all her *toys*, as she calls them—a floor full of kayaks, paddleboards, and floaties shaped like unicorns and doughnuts. Out the back, there is a Zodiac inflatable motorboat on a mechanical arm "to take us to the island later," she tells us. We move down to the rear deck, and I am stunned to see it has its own outdoor pool and hot tub. This is so different from the escape-room and laser-tag birthdays parties I'm used to. I'm sure my friends back home have never seen anything like this. I feel a slight pain in my side and take a sip of the ginger tea to make it go away.

"Third deck is strictly off-limits," she says. "My parents and their friends are up there. But there's a sauna and a movie theater belowdeck. You guys, this is going to be a blast, and I'm so glad you're all here to celebrate with me!"

Everyone cheers and then takes off to explore.

As we cruise into the open sea, the water becomes choppier. I move to the front deck of the boat so I can have the wind on my face and I sip my tummy-calming tea, thankful for Joy's foresight. I seem to have the right idea, because a few others come to join me, like Rosie, Henry, and Theo. From here, the sea looks like it goes on forever. We pass a few container ships, some sailboats, and a giant yacht with a helipad. I can't believe there's an even bigger boat than Gemma's.

When Dev sits beside me, Theo moves to sit with Jinsae, who has just parked himself across the deck from us.

"It doesn't seem like you guys are good friends," I say loud enough for Dev to hear me, but soft enough to be muffled by the wind to the others.

"We used to be," he says as he gives a wistful glance toward Theo and Jinsae.

"Really? What happened?"

"The Science Cup." Dev looks down at his hands and furrows his eyebrows.

"What do you mean?"

"Last year, we had this big Lower School science fair with a prize award and everything. We built a machine together that could automatically pass hockey balls so I could practice first-timing it into the net."

"That sounds awesome."

"The coaches and PE department loved it. The soccer coach even asked us to make a prototype that could pass soccer balls."

"Well…" I tread gingerly "…what was the problem?"

"There was a big school ceremony to present the Science Cup prizes. My whole family came. But then Mr. Gregg only called Theo onstage, like he was the only person who did the project. I kept waiting for Theo to correct him and invite me onstage, but he just stood there and took all the credit. Then it was over and too late to say anything."

"Have you tried to talk to him about it? Ask him what happened? Maybe work things out."

"Nah, our friendship is done."

I want to argue, but am not sure what to say. I think back to my argument with Natalie. Is that what she was thinking about me, that it was *done*? That we were *done*? For a few seconds, I'm a little sad, but then I look out to the sea and back over the massive yacht full of my laughing and smiling classmates and think how amazing my life in Hong Kong is, and I swipe all thoughts of home overboard, to be lost at sea.

When the boat slows and the choppiness subsides, we move to the pool area, and people start taking off their outer layers. The girls are all wearing cute bikinis in a rainbow of colors and mix of styles. Even Rosie has a bandeau top on with a pretty daisy pattern. I'm wearing the racer-back one-piece I bought with her. Even if I wanted to wear a bikini, there's no way Mom would ever let me. She says I need to wait until I'm older.

Rosie and I sit on fancy beanbag chairs with built-in cupholders, in which we put our cans of limonata.

"So…" I say, poking her arm. "I saw you and Henry talking just now. I think he has a crush on you."

Rosie's cheeks go all pink. "Do you really think?"

"For sure," I say. "Are you going to ask him to hang out?"

"Oh, no, I could never say something first." She giggles and twirls her long blond hair around her finger.

Gemma struts by, drinking from a coconut with a silver straw, and I call out to her. Might as well get it over with.

"Hey, Gemma." I scramble up to go after her. "Happy birthday."

I pull a wrapped present from my backpack and hand it to her. She rips open the paper and crumples it up into a ball.

"A book. Thanks," she says a little flatly.

"It's my all-time favorite book. *Anne of Green Gables*," I say proudly. A Canadian classic. I just love how Anne Shirley is so strong and fearless, even though she sometimes gets in trouble.

"Oh, goody. I can't wait to read it."

I can't tell if she means it or not, and I don't have time to ask because someone behind me catches her eye. It's Theo watching us from the other side of the deck, with a package in his hand. She bounds over to him, tossing my gift on the table stacked high with unopened ones, and gives him a hug.

"A gift? You shouldn't have! I explicitly said no gifts."

I laugh under my breath at the difference in her reaction.

"It's nothing really, but I thought you might enjoy it," he says.

She looks at the package, a rectangle, wrapped in blue paper, Tiffany blue. Her eyes are wide with anticipation. "Whatever could this be?" She rips the paper open and, for a millisecond, I see her surprise register. Disappointed surprise, but soon it's replaced by a smile.

"Another book. Fantastic. I *love* to read," she says. But the upper half of her face doesn't move when she smiles, a sure sign that she is faking. I hear Theo say something about an autographed copy of one of the Harry Potter books, which sounds super cool. I wonder what she was expecting in the blue box? A tiara?

We anchor in a turquoise bay in front of a small uninhabited island with a sandy beach. The crew inflates a giant slide that goes from the top deck down the starboard side to the water. The yacht has to be several stories high, and the slide is at a steep pitch. No wonder Theo was so excited about it. We all gather at the top and look down. The clear blue water sparkles in the sunlight, beckoning us in. Rhys and Jinsae jostle for position at the front of the line.

Finally, Jinsae dekes to the side and leaps over Rhys to go down the slide headfirst.

"Oooh, this looks too fast for me," Rosie says.

"What about you, Holly-Mei?" Theo asks.

As brave as I want to seem, I'm not ready just yet. "I think I'll watch a few others go down first."

Rainbow scoffs, gently mocking us. "Don't be such chickens!" and then leaps onto the slide, screaming all the way down.

When it's my turn, the drop takes my breath away. It's exhilarating, more so than any roller coaster I've ever been on. But I forget to close my eyes when I hit the water, and the stinging of the salt is intensely painful when I surface.

"Here." Snowy hands me a hose as I climb the ladder onto the sea-level deck. "Flush your eyes out." I squirt the cool water onto my face and feel immediate relief.

"Thanks," I say. "I forgot the water would be salty."

"The slide's too high," Snowy says. "Both times I went down, I hit the water like I was belly flopping."

I wince. That must have hurt way more than my eyes.

After watching more people go down, Snowy says, "Let's find Rainbow. I heard her and Rosie say they wanted to try one of those." She points down at a giant floating foam mat bobbing up and down with the waves. "There's another one farther down that I bet they're on now."

We walk to the stern and down a set of stairs to the water, where Rosie, Rainbow, and Lizzie, in her big straw sunhat, are lounging on the other foam mat.

"What do we do?" I ask.

"Try not to fall off." Snowy laughs.

I step on it, and it seems easy enough.

"And if you do, don't forget to close your eyes," Snowy says.

Suddenly we hear a chorus of "Cannonball!" and four big, curled-up bodies land in the water, spraying the five of us. Theo, Jinsae, Rhys, and Dev all clamber onto the mat, making it unstable. We're all standing now, trying to shake each other off. The mat wobbles, and I lose my footing but quickly recover it. Rhys also falters, grabbing Lizzie's arm to stabilize himself, and they both fall in. Luckily Lizzie's hat floats.

"Last one standing is the boss!" Dev says.

One by one, people topple in. I bend my knees slightly and tighten my core so I can balance better. After Theo knocks Jinsae in, it's just me, him, and Dev left on the mat. We dance around each other to the sound of cheering. Dev lunges at me like he's going in for a slide rugby tackle, but I jump to the side, and he barely manages to avoid slipping off the mat.

"Hey, go easy on her," Theo says.

"What? Why?" I ask, my hands on my hips.

"Holly-Mei can handle herself," Dev says.

"You said it," I yell as I make a running jump toward the middle of the mat, landing so hard the mat ripples and the two boys fly off either corner. I put my arms up in a victory salute as Rosie and the girls cry, "Woo-hoo, Holly-Mei!"

We pile into the Zodiac that will shuttle us to the island for a picnic lunch on the beach. The crew has set up a barbecue and is grilling burgers and pouring drinks. As Rosie and I sit on the peachy-pink sand eating cheeseburgers, we can see Gemma's parents and their friends on the top deck of the boat.

"I wonder why they're not down here with us. It's her birthday, after all," I say.

"I guess her parents are hands-off, except when it comes to being pushy," Rosie says wryly.

We lie back, stuffed, and listen to the sounds of the breeze in the trees and the beat of the waves. I feel myself relax and realize I haven't thought about our presentation all day. Snowy and Rainbow are more fun than I thought they'd be. With Gemma busy being queen of the day, they've spent the last few hours hanging out with Rosie and me. Rainbow loves sports as much as I do, but she's more into skiing and horseback riding, and Snowy doesn't just like to be on-screen, she takes action shots throughout the day on her camera.

Out of the corner of my eye, I see Henry nearby, and when Snowy gets up, he jumps and takes her spot beside Rosie.

Rainbow nudges me with her elbow. "Let's go get a sundae." She points to the ice-cream bar set up over by the palm trees.

"I'm good," I say, patting my stomach.

"They have sprinkles. Come help me choose which kind," Rainbow says as she gets up.

Now it clicks. Rainbow wants to leave Henry and Rosie to chat. I take the hint and follow her.

"Oh, you're going, too?" Rosie's cheeks become a pale shade of pink.

"Don't worry. Now you can finally be alone with Henry," I say with a giggle.

Rosie's smile fades, and her cheeks turn from pink to crimson. Oh, bummer, I just did that blurting thing again. Henry tries to hide a laugh, but she looks embarrassed. And angry. I've never seen her frown with lines so deep before. She puts on a smile, the same kind Gemma had before—just with the lower part of her face—and asks Rainbow to get her a sundae, too.

By midafternoon, Rosie is still ignoring me. Some people stay on the island, some continue to play in the water, and some, including me, head back to the boat, which is thankfully moored in calm waters. To escape the sun, I head to a sheltered deck and sit in the shade. Rosie and Henry are in a double kayak in the distance, and Theo's off on his own on the paddleboard. Rhys and a group of guys yell and scream in the water with a makeshift game of water rugby. Rainbow and Snowy are on a floating mat.

Nestled on a beanbag with a stomach full of ice cream, my eyes slowly fall shut. I'm not sure how long

I've been dozing when I hear someone's piercing shriek: "Rainbow? Oh my God! *Rainbow!*"

I jolt up, feeling like someone slapped me across the face. For a minute, I can't remember where I am, but when I hear Rainbow's name screamed again, I race down the stairs, running over to the side of the yacht where a small crowd of people start to gather. Snowy is alone on the mat, tears streaming down her face.

"I don't know where she is!" she cries. "We were on the mat, and she fell in when she tried to get up."

I scan the water and make out a dark shape under the far edge of the foam mat. The second that registers, I jump in. Someone else jumps in beside me.

I open my eyes and ignore the stinging of the salt. The dark shape isn't her, it's just a shadow. I come up for air and go down again under the mat. This time I see her, by the side of the boat. I swim over and see her bikini tie tangled around some sort of hook. Her eyes are closed, and she's not moving. My heart skips a beat. I put my lips to hers and blow the contents of my lungs into her mouth. Theo appears beside me, and we grab her under the arms and roughly yank her up, ripping her bathing suit with the force. Together, we pull her upward and gasp for air when

195

we break through to the surface. Someone above us grabs Rainbow and pulls her onto the mat. It's Dev.

"It's okay, I've got her now," he says. He lays her onto the mat, checks for breathing, and puts her in recovery position. Everyone audibly sighs with relief as she starts to cough water up.

"Stuck...couldn't...up..." she says between coughs.

Jinsae wraps a towel around her, picks her up, and carries her back onto the boat.

"Well done," Theo says. "That was really brave of you."

"You, too," I say. "I guess you know now that I can handle myself."

"Beyond any doubt," he says with a faint smile.

Everyone moves back inside the boat, except Snowy, frozen in place.

"Hey." I climb back onto the mat and sit down beside her. "It's okay now. She's going to be okay."

Snowy gives me a weak smile before bursting into tears again. "I thought she'd drowned."

"I know. It was super scary. I was scared, too."

I wrap my arms around her. I know how she feels. When we were really young, Millie was climbing a tree in our backyard when she stepped on a cracked branch. She fell to the ground with a thud and got the wind knocked out of her, but I had been convinced for a second that she was dying. It was the most terrifying second of my life.

"It's all going to be fine," I say soothingly as I rub her back. I don't even flinch when she vomits on my leg.

The crew turns the yacht around shortly after that, and we begin the trip back to the marina club. I think there was supposed to be dinner and a cake and some dancing, but Rainbow's near-death experience put a damper on the rest of the party. But if Gemma's upset, it doesn't show. She's going around making sure everyone's comfortable, directing the crew to bring out more towels and serve snacks, even though I heard her mother scold her for us kids "not being more responsible." Maybe if her parents were around more this wouldn't have happened.

Snowy goes to find Rainbow, and I search belowdeck for an empty stateroom. I go into the first one I find and take a long hot shower in its marble-tiled bathroom. When I finally feel clean again, I turn the water off and wrap myself in an impossibly fluffy towel hanging from the warm rack. When I step out into the room, Gemma is lying on the king-size bed, staring up at the crystal seashell light fixture.

"Hi, Gemma," I say cautiously. "Sorry, is this your room?"

"No." She sits up. "I was waiting for you. I wanted to

say thank-you, Holly-Mei. The way you dove into the ocean like that—it was awesome. And, just, thank you. I know I should say more, but I don't know what else to say."

"No need to thank me," I say. "It's over, and she's okay. That's all that matters."

"How much would that have ruined my party if she weren't?" she asks.

I don't say anything, unsure whether this is what Mom calls *dry British humor.*

"I'm joking." She laughs, and I relax. "Rainbow is fine, and she's being doted on by Snowy and Rosie. My dad called her parents, and they're bringing her to the hospital to get checked out."

We sit in silence for a minute, and she examines the hem of her embroidered caftan.

"It's pretty," I say.

"Thanks. I designed and sewed it myself. I want to be a fashion designer one day."

"That sounds pretty cool," I say.

"My parents don't think so. It's not on the list of acceptable professions," Gemma scoffs.

"Wait, let me guess. Doctor, lawyer, engineer, or banker?" I ask, laughing.

"My parents expect me and my brother to take over

the family business." She lets out a big exhale, then gathers herself and smiles. "Are your parents pushy like that, too?"

"I'm bracing myself. But at least we're only in Grade 7. We've got plenty of time."

Gemma nods, but her smile is tight, and I notice she bites her lip like she wants to say more. I wait for it, but she doesn't say anything.

One of the crew members shouts, "Docking in five!" and Gemma starts to leave.

"I better get back upstairs," she says. "I've got to calm my mother down. She's annoyed her day on the boat with friends has been cut short."

"Yes, sure," I say as if I understand, but I really can't. I feel like I've seen a new side of Gemma, one that I really like, and another side of Hong Kong life, one that I really don't.

15

On Monday we have the day off from school, so we pile into our van to head to the border for a day trip to shop in Shenzhen—a favorite pastime of Auntie Helen's. I had envisaged that my first-ever trip to Mainland China would involve hiking the Great Wall, exploring the Forbidden Palace in Beijing, or visiting the Terracotta Warriors in Xi'an. But no such luck. The ride to the Chinese border is long and unusually quiet. Ah-Lok, our driver, is in the front on his own. He's driving us because he has some special cross-border license plate that Rosie's driver doesn't have. Auntie Helen and Tinsley, the American lady from next door, are sitting in the middle row, and Rosie, Millie, and I are in the back. Rosie isn't talking to me. She's not even looking at me. And she hasn't responded to any of my texts. I don't know what to do. I'm sure she thinks I embarrassed her on purpose, but it just popped out of my mouth. I wish I could have one of those time-delays like they do on the radio so I could press a button to catch things that I forget to filter.

After the border crossing, I notice that we are driving on the other side of the road, like we do in Canada, rather than the Hong Kong/British right-hand side, so Ah-Lok's steering wheel is on the wrong side. That's not the only eye-opener. The city feels more surreal than Hong Kong, a sea of glass towers and wide, tree-lined streets, but no pedestrians. It's eerily quiet.

"I thought you said Shenzhen was dumpy," Millie says to Auntie Helen.

"The mall we're going to is a right dump, but it's brill, you'll see. And all this is new and flash." Helen points out the window.

Tinsley pipes in as she turns and flips her aviator sunglasses onto her head. "This is one of China's richest cities. Thirty years ago, it was a small fishing village. Imagine that! Now it's a city of twelve million people. Much bigger than Hong Kong."

I look around at all the buildings and can't believe how fast the city has popped up. I wonder what happened to the people who lived here before they started building. Are they now in these gleaming towers?

We drive past a couple of fancy brand-name hotels and stop at what looks like a low-rise office building, with a neon sign on top that says *Luohu*. There are people gathered outside smoking, shielding their eyes from the reflection of the sun off the dirty mirrored cladding.

"We're here!" Auntie Helen says in a singsongy voice. "Get into your shopping mode. Let's start at the fabric market. You all brought some clothes you want copied, right? Mrs. Ming's seamstresses can make anything, even from a picture cut out of a magazine."

Inside the mall feels like an indoor flea market, except every stall has its own glass walls. As we walk by, people yell *Sunglasses*, *Prada*, *iPhone*, trying to lure us into their businesses. As we ride up the escalator to the fifth floor, we can see shops selling shoes, bags, glasses, and electronics.

The market is filled with thousands of bolts of fabric standing on end. It's like the board of the Candy Land game come to life—a sanctuary from the stale smells and clamor of the floors below. It reminds me of shopping at Fabric Ville with Ah-ma back home when she would let me and Millie pick a Butterick pattern and she would make us matching dresses.

We find Mrs. Ming's stall at the back of the market. She seems to be popular with foreigners, as indicated by the photos of ladies dressed in their newly tailored clothes under the glass of her stall counter. We pull out what we brought. Auntie Helen and her friend have a pile of dresses and blouses they want copied and custom-tailored. I brought the linen dress I wore to the welcome party, Rosie's hand-me-down. Mrs. Ming brings us to a fabric stall, and the lady there promptly shows us a variety of fabrics that would work for our clothes. I pick a bright red, something other than the dull gray of my original dress, to brighten up my dull mood.

I can't stand walking on eggshells around Rosie anymore. My heart is bursting to know if she's going to stay mad at me forever. I try to make a joke and see if she'll take my olive branch. "Red, like your cheeks yesterday." I hold up the fabric close to my face.

She looks at me wide-eyed and then bursts out laughing.

"I'm so, so sorry," I say. "I wasn't trying to embarrass you."

"I know you meant well, but I wanted to tell him on my terms, not yours." She pauses a second before continuing in a gentle tone. "Holly-Mei, maybe just take a second from when a thought pops in your head to when words come out of your mouth?"

Harsh. I want to retort, tell her she's wrong, and defend myself, but I take her advice and wait a second before speaking. Then the rush of words that want to spill out of my mouth slowly evaporates. I nod and say, "I'm working on it."

She reaches over and gives me a hug, and the knot in my stomach disappears and is replaced by butterflies—excitement not only that I fixed things with her, but that maybe other friendships are fixable. My mind flits to Theo and Dev. Maybe I can help them become friends again, too.

"The red suits your tanned skin," Rosie says. "Why don't you get a second one made in another color since we're here?"

"Not a bad idea," I say.

Mrs. Ming quotes me one hundred yuan renminbi for a copy, including fabric. That's about the price of four bubble teas. Dad gave me and Millie six hundred yuan spending money each, so I'll have plenty left over if I get two dresses. Even after walking through the maze of fabrics over and over, I still can't decide between black and navy. I try and rope in Millie to help. She had already beelined it to the fabric she wanted to use to copy her miniskirt—leopard-print—and now she's sitting on a red plastic stool at Mrs. Ming's counter staring at her dataless phone.

"Get the black—it's easier to accessorize." Millie lets out a big sigh. "I'm *so* bored. We've been looking at fabrics for almost an hour, and there's no Wi-Fi here!"

Auntie Helen is standing in front of the mirror being measured by Mrs. Ming.

"Rosie, darling," she says, "why don't you walk around with the girls and meet us back here in an hour? Then we'll have lunch before moving on to handbags."

Relieved to be getting away from this stuffy corner of the mall, we take off to explore.

"I can't remember which is Mum's favorite shoe shop," Rosie says as we walk by several identical shops selling identical fakes.

"No worries. Let's just go in here." I open the door to the nearest one.

The shelves are lined with all the latest designer shoes, and Millie squeals with delight when she sees a pair of white sneakers with green and red stripes and a bee embroidered on with golden thread.

"Hols, I just have to have those. They're Gucci!"

I scoff, "Get real. They're fake."

"Well, they're super cute."

Millie looks at the saleslady and asks, "Duo shao qian?" *How much?* She turns to us and says, "I guess my Chinese will come in handy after all."

The lady types twelve hundred into the calculator. I'm not really into shopping, but I get caught up in the excitement of bargain hunting. "One thousand two hundred yuan? That's way too expensive! Tai gui le."

The lady hands me the calculator, and I type in four hundred. Ah-ma taught us how to bargain at the markets in Taiwan when we went to visit family. The lady retypes six hundred in the calculator. Millie nods, and the lady hands a box to her. As she opens it, her eyes light up like it's Christmas morning.

"Hols, you might have to buy me lunch and the skirt, I've spent all the money Dad gave me." Millie giggles as she counts out her red one-hundred-yuan notes. She puts her flip-flops in her bag and her new shoes on. She parades down the hall like she's on a catwalk. It reminds me of the fashion-designer talk I had with Gemma. I wonder what she would think of this trip, all these fakes.

"Oh, let's go in here," I say, approaching an optical shop. I try on a pair of pink heart-shaped sunglasses with pink lenses.

"Those look great. How do they look on me?" Millie asks, taking another heart-shaped pair from the salesperson.

"Super cute. Rosie, try them on, too," I say, handing her an identical pair.

"Let's all get them," she says as we giggle at our triplet reflection.

I pay for Millie's, and she jumps up and down with glee.

I guess the saying is right: everything looks brighter, happier, with rose-tinted glasses on.

Millie wants to keep trying on more glasses, but I am famished.

"I'm going to fall over if I don't get some food into me. I'll quickly grab something and meet you back here, okay?"

"Sure, we won't move far," Rosie says.

I head down three sets of escalators on my hunt for snacks since I remember seeing something when we walked in earlier. On the ground floor, I find a shop selling big bags of chips, but realize when I pick it up it's a bag of dried braised duck necks. I'm an adventurous eater, but that seems a bit much for a midmorning snack. I keep looking until I find a lady with a table laden with fruit: branches of lychees, shiny red mountain apples, and yellow baby bananas, no longer than my finger. I opt for a juicy green guava. I wipe it clean with water and tissue from my bag, take a big crunchy bite, and savor the sweet but tart flavor.

My stomach rumblings subside, and I head back up the escalator to the third floor. When I step off, nothing looks familiar. I walk by the same glass-walled stalls over and over. Or are they different stalls selling the same things? The air feels stuffy and like the ceiling is getting lower each corner I turn. I feel like I'm trapped in a funfair crazy house. I sit on a plastic stool outside a stall and pull out my phone. Maybe I can text Millie. But then I remember I have no Wi-Fi or roaming. I sit back and lean against the glass, its coldness easing my throbbing head.

I try not to panic, but my hands are clammy, and dark

thoughts creep into my head. What if I don't find them? What if I get stuck here in Mainland China, all alone? But am I not almost all alone back in Hong Kong? My mom wants to take away my field hockey. My only real friend is my cousin, whom I almost managed to completely alienate. I sort of have friends in Rainbow and Snowy, Theo and Dev, but none that I can just call up and fully be myself without worrying whether I'm going to mess things up. My plan for moving seemed so perfect, and I'm annoyed and mad—or make that sad—that nothing is as smooth as I expected. I get up and start walking again, and I head to the escalators.

Then I hear it. Someone shouting my name. "Yo, Hols! Up here!" It's Millie waving with both arms in the air. I run up the escalators and almost collapse in her arms.

"Where were you guys?" I ask with panting breaths.

"We've been here all along," Rosie says.

"No, you guys changed floors," I say. "I left you on the third floor."

"Nope, this is the fourth floor," Millie says.

"No, I walked down three flights to the ground floor from the third floor."

"There is no ground floor here, like they have in Hong

209

Kong. They call it the first floor, so you came up a floor short," Rosie explains.

All this panic and wasted time over a simple mis-understanding.

16

After a long van ride back from the border, I need to stretch my legs and breathe some fresh air, so I head down to the grocery store at the base of our complex. I'm going to pick up some ice cream for dessert—cookies and cream for Millie and Mom, and chocolate mint for me and Dad.

Just before I step into the shop, I see Dev heading around the corner. I catch up to him. "Hey, wait up," I say as he is opening the door to a store tucked in the corner of the shopping arcade. He gives me a big hello and a smile and holds the door open for me. I step inside. It's a bookshop, small and cramped, heaving with books and stationery and a wall of candy imported from all over the world. It's so bright inside despite the increasing number of ominous-looking clouds outside.

"Are you looking for something in particular?" I ask.

"*The Hobbit*. I've seen the film, but thought I should try the book. My grandma gave me a gift card for my birthday in the summer, and I haven't gotten around to using it."

"Oh, thanks for the reminder. I need to pick up a card," I say as I walk toward the birthday card selection. I find a really cute one that says *Happy Birthday, Sweet Tart*, with a drawing of two egg custard tarts. "My grandma will love this," I say.

"Is she back in Canada?" Dev asks.

I nod.

"That must be tough. My nani lives on the same street as me. You must miss yours a lot."

"More than I thought I would. I can't really talk to my mom in the same way as I can talk to her. And plus, it seems like my mom has changed since coming here." I shrug and walk toward the book section.

"It's a big deal to move countries, let alone continents. You okay?"

"Totally great."

"Really?" he asks gently.

"Well, maybe not great, but okay. I thought it would be easier, you know, like a perfect start in perfect new city."

"It sounds like your expectations should be over there." He points to a shelf of books. It's the fairy-tale section.

"Ha-ha, very funny," I say.

"At least I made you laugh. You've been here, like, what, a month? You can't expect it to be perfect right away."

I nod, digesting what he just said. Maybe it's okay for it not to be perfect.

I get a familiar whiff of raspberry goodness as Dev rips open a pack of Twizzlers and offers me a stick before putting it on the cashier's counter along with his book.

"My favorite!" I say.

"Mine, too."

The rain lashes at the window on Tuesday morning, waking me up before my alarm goes off. The sky is still dark as I make my way to the kitchen. Millie is already there pouring corn flakes into her bowl and intently refreshing an app on her phone.

"What are you doing?" My question is mangled within my yawn.

"I'm checking on the typhoon signal. It's T3 right now."

I shrug as I peel my banana. "So?"

"So, if the government raises the alert to T8, we get the day off school. Lizzie told me that we'll know by six thirty."

That would be two days in a row of no school! I look at the clock on the microwave. Six twenty-nine flashes in bright green.

Both our phones ping.

"Yesss! T8!" Millie dances around the kitchen.

An alert from school fills my screen stating school is canceled according to the government weather guidelines. I guess it's like having a snow day, but somehow the prospect of playing outside in a hurricane seems a lot less fun.

"Woo-hoo! Typhoon day! I'm totally going back to bed." Millie dumps her cereal into the sink.

"Aren't you two lucky?" Dad walks into the kitchen. He

puts the kettle on. "The university library is closed today, so my research has to wait. Anyone for tea?"

"Sure," I say.

Dad and I sit at the dining table sharing a pot of Earl Grey. He salts his soft-boiled egg while I spread peanut butter on my toast.

"We rarely get a quiet moment like this." He passes me the sections of the New York Times he's finished reading so I can flip through.

"You okay, poppet? How's school?"

"It's fine."

He lays down his paper and looks at me with concern on his face.

"Want to talk about it?"

"No," I say, "but thanks, Dad."

"Patience, darling, we just got here," he says as if he could read my mind.

We sit in silence with nothing but the sound of crunchy toast and the turning of the newspaper pages.

"Your mother's lucky she flew to Tokyo last night," Dad says as he looks out the window.

The day off school brings with it some culinary delights, as Joy teaches Millie how to make some Filipino specialties—pancit, a rice noodle stir-fry with tender chicken chunks; eggplant adobo with its special vinegar soy sauce; and bibingka, a rice-flour cake made with creamy coconut milk. And I get to taste them all.

Late afternoon, the doorbell rings. It's Tinsley from across the hall. She hands me a giant brown paper bag from Bloomingdale's, overflowing with stuff.

"I was clearing out our closets today. I'm going to donate these clothes and shoes, but thought you and your sister might want to look through them. You can give away what you don't want," she says. "They're all in good condition, but it's stuff Aisling has outgrown or we don't wear anymore. The handbags are all Shenzhen specials," she says with a wink.

I thank her profusely and run to my room, my arms tightly wrapped around the precious cargo. I love the idea of going green and recycling. Like Dad says, someone's rubbish is another's treasure. I never thought I'd be excited about clothes, but ever since Rosie handed down some clothes to me, I have been a bit more curious about wearing things other than sportswear. It feels like Christmas has come early. I dump the contents onto my bed: there were more clothes in that bag than I have in all my drawers combined. A rainbow of colors, soft and shiny fabrics. I call Millie to come to my room. She picks up some sparkly flats and tries them on. "I looove them. They're a touch big, but I'll grow into them." She claps her hands with glee.

I try on an emerald-green short-sleeve silk wrap dress.

"What do you think?" I twirl around.

"That color looks really nice on you."

"You think?" Would Theo smile with those dimples if he ever saw me in it? Or would Dev flash me that mega-watt smile?

"Yes. You look very pretty in that dress. I might have to steal it." She laughs.

We each take a few more things from the pile. I end up with a handful of casual dresses and some simple black suede ballet flats that will go nicely with new my tailored dresses from Shenzhen. Luckily Tinsley's daughter is the same shoe size as me. I also take a cream-colored cashmere sweater that I put on straight away. I can't stop running my hands over the sleeves. It's the softest thing I've ever felt, like I'm touching a cloud. Cozy and safe, like everything is going to be okay.

Back at school, the teachers pile on the work, so our unexpected day off turned out to not be such a holiday after all. At lunchtime, people are still whispering about what happened with Rainbow on the boat over the weekend, even though it was days ago. I notice a lot more people are smiling at me when we pass in the hallway.

On my way to the bus, I see Dev standing in front of the trophy case in the main lobby. It looks like he's staring at the big silver trophy with the microscope on top. The Science Cup. I wonder if this is the prize from the ceremony he missed out on. His eyes look downcast. There must be something I can do to help him and Theo solve their differences. Before I can walk over and say something, Snowy and Rainbow yell my name and run toward me. Dev looks up, gives me a wave, and walks away.

"Hey, Holly-Mei, wait up," Snowy says, slightly out of breath.

Rainbow pulls a small drawstring pouch from her pocket and hands it to me. "Here, it's just a small thing to say thank-you. I made it myself."

I open the pouch, and a beaded bracelet falls into my hand.

"It's gorgeous. Thank you." I slip the cobalt-blue beads over my wrist.

"It's lapis lazuli. It represents courage," Rainbow says. I finger the beads gently.

"And the bird," Snowy says, pointing to the one gold bead among the sea of blue, "is a phoenix. For strength."

"And you really fit with the Earth House. Those who are Earth element are said to be dependable and loyal. What you did on Saturday on the boat was the mark of a true friend," Rainbow says.

"Wow, this is too nice. It means so much." We group hug.

The words *true friend* spin in my head as I spin the bracelet around my wrist. Maybe, just maybe, things are beginning to look sweeter.

17

I finally get up the nerve to do it. I lock myself in Mom's bathroom and rummage in her drawers. I've never even thought about stuff like this before. It's not like I have caterpillar brows. But looking closer with Mom's magnifying mirror, there are quite a few stray hairs. I'm annoyed that Gemma said what she did the other day on the ferry. And I'm even more annoyed that I'm starting to agree with her. Now every time I look at my eyebrows, I want to pull those few hairs out. I reach up to my brow with Mom's stainless-steel tweezers, which feel cool against my skin. I grab one of the hairs, pinch, and pull. *Oh my God!* I scream in my head. If that was the searing pain for one itty bitty hair, how am I ever going to pluck more? My trembling hand reaches for another hair, but I can't do it.

A minute later I hear a loud knock on the door.

"What are you doing in there?" Millie asks. "Are you okay? I heard a scream."

"I didn't realize I screamed out loud," I say. I open the door, tweezers in hand, my right eyebrow surrounded by red, swollen skin.

Millie shakes her head and grabs the tweezers. "You're being too rough. Come here." She pats the edge of the bathtub and motions for me to sit down. She finds a YouTube video on eyebrows, and we watch it together.

"You already have a good shape," she says after inspecting more closely. "You just need to tidy."

"You think?" I hold my breath as she pulls a few more hairs out. It's so much less painful when she does it.

"All done." She taps some moisturizer around my eyebrows to soothe the skin. "Do you want me to teach you how to apply concealer and mascara?" One of Millie's favorite pastimes, other than cooking or watching cooking shows, is to watch makeup tutorials. I shake my head. She rolls Mom's mascara tube between her thumb and fingers.

"Do you think Mom will let me start wearing makeup to school?"

"No way." I laugh at her naivety. "Maybe when you're sixteen. More likely eighteen."

She passes me the mirror. I have to admit that I look a little more sophisticated. I take a photo of my new look and send it to Rosie. I bet she'll send me back the eye-roll emoji. And maybe the starry-eyed emoji. I even wonder what Natalie would think. She'd probably laugh at me, wondering what's gotten into me since moving to Hong Kong. But I guess I won't ever know.

There's a math pop quiz first period the next day. Not my ideal start to the morning. I wish it were a pop quiz on Hong Kong history. I feel like I could ace that after our museum trip. Instead, it's a review of probabilities. If there are five green balls and seven red balls, what is the probability of getting a B+ on this quiz? I dismiss the thought of how that might disappoint my parents.

At lunch, I comfort myself with a bowl of wonton noodle soup, which I greedily slurp down as soon as I get to the table, not waiting for anyone else to arrive before I start.

"Who had math with Ms. Gurung this morning?" Jinsae asks as he and Rhys sit down with steaming plates of chicken korma with puffy naan bread on the side.

"I did," I say between spoonfuls of warm broth.

"Great. Pop quiz, I hear. Come on, give us a hint," Rhys says as he dips his naan bread into his sauce and shoves it in his mouth.

"No way. That's cheating," I say. Isn't it? In the wake of what happened at Maple Grove and the aftershocks I felt, I'm not so sure anymore.

"Of course it's cheating." Rosie arrives with her tray. "Back off, you two." She shoos the boys away farther down the table and sits in their place.

I'm relieved that I've managed to get out of that situation. Sometimes I feel like I haven't read the rules of life and don't know where I can get a copy.

Maybe Rosie knows more than me. I take an extra long time to chew my noodles so I can phrase my question just right. "What would you do if Rhys and Jinsae found out the questions and looked up the answers before the pop quiz?" I ask. "Hypothetically, of course."

"I'd be annoyed."

"Annoyed enough to blurt out something to a teacher without thinking?" I ask.

223

"Maybe. Why, did that happen to you?"

Why does she assume I did something? I guess it's because my track record is littered with the consequences of my blurting. I keep my eyes averted. I take one of the cherry tomatoes off her Greek salad and pop it in my mouth and garble something that sounds like *Uh-huh*.

After I swallow the tomato I say, "Rules. How bendy are they?" Ah-ma likes to say we have to follow the rules because the nail that sticks out gets hammered down, which sounds a bit harsh to me. But maybe there's room for flexibility. "Like, is there some sort of code we're supposed to know about?"

She laughs and says, "That's a good way of looking at it. But it's not written down. We just need to figure things out as we go." She furrows her brow and asks, "What happened after, you know, the blurting?"

"People got angry. Friends got angry." My shoulders slump a little.

"Lots of time has passed. Maybe it's time to reach out." Rosie smiles warmly and gives my hand a little squeeze. "Come on, let's grab a mango smoothie before class starts."

The costumes designed by Gemma have been ordered from a tailor, and the set designed by Rainbow is being built by the school's Performing Arts department. We have hashed out our script with bits of all our families' stories and are just tweaking the final few lines of dialogue for the section about our tragic but moving love story.

"Everyone will be on their feet at the end of our performance," Snowy says.

"Definitely a standing ovation," Rainbow says.

"Yes, it's fine." Gemma has been a bit glum ever since our trip to the museum.

"Where's Theo? He'd better not be out playing rugby while I'm stuck here," Rhys says.

"He texted to say he had an appointment and he'd be here, just a little late." Gemma taps her Apple watch and lets out a little huff.

Snowy practices her curtsy. "You know, for when I'm on Broadway or winning my Oscar."

"I thought you wanted to be a YouTuber," I say.

"After practicing on stage, I might join the drama club. Do some *Shakespeare*," she says the last word in a mock-posh British accent.

The late bell rings, and we head out into the hallway. Theo runs over, out of breath. "Sorry I'm late. I thought I'd be here sooner."

"No problem, Theo," Gemma says with an ear-to-ear grin, although she seemed a little annoyed at him just a minute ago.

"I actually have something to show you guys," Theo says.

As we gather around him, I see Dev Singh at his locker looking over. Theo reaches into his bag and pulls out a black box. He gently places it on the top of a nearby table. The box looks like a hard-plastic briefcase. He turns the numbers of the built-in lock, and it opens with a loud click. I don't know what I expected to see inside, but it certainly wasn't a jade necklace, more brilliant and vivid than when it was in the glass box at the museum.

"Is it—?" Gemma's mouth hangs open. It's probably the first time that she's ever been at a loss for words.

"Yes. My dad arranged to let me borrow it for the performance Saturday. It's from our family collection. It's supposed to be locked in the safe at home."

Gemma jumps up and throws her arms around Theo.

226

"You are amazing, Theo Fitzwilliam-Lo. Our performance will be the best of the night."

Theo smiles modestly, looking a little uncomfortable with all the attention.

"Getting ready to take all the glory again, eh, Theo?" Dev asks from across the hallway, stony-faced.

Theo snaps the lid of the case shut. "Dev, you don't know what you're talking about."

Dev looks at us and says, "Expect him to take all the credit." Then he gives Theo a hard stare and swings his backpack over his shoulder and walks off, his head high.

I wait for Theo to say something back, defend himself somehow, but he stays quiet, although Rhys and Gemma are chattering away with "What's his problem?" and "He's just jealous of how good we're going to be." Theo jams the case back in his bag and says he needs to run for the bus and get home before his mother notices the case isn't in the safe anymore.

This is ridiculous. I'm going to help them make up and become friends again.

I change into my PE kit and walk over to the field hockey pitch to hit some balls. Just as I had hoped, Dev is there shooting at the goalie. I want to talk to him about the science fair incident and why he dislikes Theo so much. I'm sure if they talked it out, they could move past it.

I grab a stick, and Dev waves me over and flashes his trademark huge smile. I immediately forget what I wanted to ask him.

"Hey, Holly-Mei, want to practice your reverse sticks again?" Dev asks.

"Sure!" I run over to the top of the D and start stretching, touching my toes, and doing some lunges. "Let's see if I can actually get them in the goal this time," I say excitedly.

Dev leads a session, teaching a few of us how to do a reverse shot on goal. He's super patient and gives us each individual tips depending on our problems. Like, for me, it's "Get lower to the ground" and to someone else, it's "Keep the ball in line with your foot" and to a complete beginner, it's "Don't swing the stick in a loop over your head." He says that last bit as the stick narrowly misses hitting him straight on the nose. By the end of the session, I'm hitting the ball in the vicinity of the goalie, and once even hearing the thunderous thud when it gets past. I've finally learned to do something I've only ever seen during Olympic matches on television or at real matches when Dad took me and Natalie to watch the University of Toronto in a derby with York University, two of the top teams in Canada.

"Hey, let me film you, so you can see what you're doing right, for next time," he says and pulls his phone from his pocket. I can't resist having my new skill on camera. He leans in to show me the footage, and I remember my plan.

"Dev, about you and Theo," I say gently. "Have you talked to him? About how you feel? You know, about the whole science project thing."

Dev looks away into the hills beyond. "No. I don't think he cares."

"Of course he does. Did you see him just now? He was embarrassed and upset."

"Well," he says, tapping his hockey stick on the ground, "that whole episode made me upset."

"Yes, but it was Mr. Gregg's mistake. And I'm sure Theo had his reasons for not correcting him in front of a whole auditorium. Maybe he was embarrassed? Or scared? But you won't know if you don't ask."

Dev doesn't say anything, but I can tell by the look on his face that he's thinking deeply about what I've just said.

"Isn't your friendship worth trying to save? You said yourself that you used to be good friends."

"We've been friends since kindergarten." He lets out a big exhale.

"I think you should reach out to him."

"I'll think about it," Dev says with a hint of a smile. "Now, eyes back on the ball. You have a lot of work to do if you want to master this new skill."

After dinner, I flip open my laptop and give Ah-ma a call.

"I have so much to tell you!" I say excitedly. I fill her in on my reverse-stick trick.

"Practice makes perfect," Ah-ma says in a singsongy voice. Even though she's never played field hockey, she has always been my biggest cheerleader.

"Well, I've also been practicing being a better friend. Listening more. And I think I've helped two friends start to make up." I tell her about Dev and Theo and the Science Cup. "I think they just need to talk to each other. Listen and communicate."

"That is nice to hear. Friendship take work. From both sides."

I twirl the end of my ponytail around my finger as I think over what she just said. *Work. From both sides.* "You know, I think maybe it's time I reach out and try and save my own friendship."

She gives me a knowing nod. "Go, baobei. Find your sweetness."

As soon as I get off the video call with Ah-ma, I pull out my phone and type in a message. My olive branch.

ME: *Hi Nat, I'm sorry for what happened. And I'm sorry I didn't say bye before moving. I miss you. HM xo*

18

The silk of my turquoise cheongsam is cool and smooth. I marvel at the embroidered flowers whose name I forget. Pansies? Poppies? Peonies? Astonishing how quickly Gemma was able to get these tailored. Maybe they were made in her dad's factory. I stick a couple of fingers in the collar and gently tug, trying to loosen it. The closer I get to Saturday night's performance, the tighter the dress feels.

I walk stiffly into the living room. Because the dress is so formfitting, I cannot take big steps.

"Oh, baby, you look beautiful," Mom says with more than a hint of surprise in her voice. She gets up and walks to me for a closer look. She tucks a stray strand of hair that's come undone from my ponytail behind my ear. "So pretty."

"Why are you walking like a robot?" Millie asks.

"There's no give in this material. I can barely move." I do a little twirl. But I can't even lift my arms up, the dress is so constrictive. "Do you think these dresses were like this on purpose? To keep women in the olden days looking pretty but not able to do much?"

"Like a corset, I suppose. Oh, poppet, you do look lovely." Dad's eyes twinkle.

"She cleans up well," Millie says. "And she'd look so much better with a bit of makeup. You know, for the stage. So maybe we can go buy some mascara at Sasa tomorrow after school?" Sasa is like the Hong Kong equivalent to Sephora, but cheap and cheerful, and with lots of Japanese and Korean brands, so Millie tells me. But one look and an arched eyebrow from Mom silences her. Millie crosses her arms and flops deeper into the sofa.

"More importantly, you know all your lines?" Mom sits up and folds her hands on her lap, all businesslike.

"Yes, of course." My tone sounds a little wounded, even though Mom is half-right to be worried. After the first disastrous rehearsal, Gemma was so exasperated at me freezing onstage and forgetting my lines, she said I could read my lines off a scroll, like a town crier, since I'm the narrator and don't have an acting part. I don't know how people can stay calm and collected on stage. At least I know that I'm never going to be an actress, and that's fine with me. And this way, I can't mess up my lines and make Mom look bad in front of everyone.

Speaking of everyone, even Tinsley Rosenblum from next door is going Saturday night. There she is, appearing behind the front door as Joy opens it. She walks into the living room *with her shoes on*. I look over at Mom, her hands gripping the edge of the sofa as Tinsley traipses outside dirt into our home.

"I just wanted to wish you luck for the upcoming Tsien Wing Opening Gala," Tinsley says, waving the gold-embossed invitation with her French-manicured hand.

"Oh, thanks. You're going?" I ask. I thought her daughter had already left the school.

"Ken and I were part of the school's annual-fund committee, and of course we were regular donors over the

234

years." She pauses and looks at Mom and Dad like she wants that information to sink in.

Tinsley eyes my dress. "I have one just like it, but in fuchsia. I need some sessions with my personal trainer so I can fit into it again." She laughs and looks me up and down. "You know, I wear it with a pair of silver chopsticks in my hair. It looks fabulous. Would you like to borrow them?"

"Um, no, thank you." I laugh at the thought of putting eating utensils in my hair.

Mom and Dad start making pleasantries with her, so I duck away and head back to my room as quickly as my constricted little steps can take me, careful not to tear the side slits. I pass Millie's room and she's in front of her full-length mirror, trying on a silver-sequinned dress.

"How does this look? I picked it up with Lizzie at a second-hand shop. I'm going to wear it Saturday night." She twirls around, and the light from the ceiling bounces off her like a disco ball. I used to envy the lightness of her steps, the lightness of her heart. If it weren't for pressure from this exhibition and the limitations of my dress, I would be twirling, too, because I when I woke up this morning, I had a text back from Natalie. *I miss you too. [Heart emoji]*

We texted back and forth until I had to catch the bus to school. I even sent her the video that Dev took.

NAT: *Cool shot. [Field hockey stick emoji] Do that move at our U of T tryouts.*

Even though it's so far away in time, we've joked about going to university together and playing for the Varsity Blues. Something inside my heart stirs at the thought our childhood dreams haven't changed for her, either.

All day my stomach is filled with anticipation and excitement, the same feeling I get right before the start of a field hockey match. Today is our final dress rehearsal. We have been doing nothing but eating and breathing this performance with all its connected pressures for almost a month. Our skit is only ten minutes long, but these ten minutes are the difference between a happy mom that will shine at work and one who will be disappointed and humiliated once again in front of very important people.

Two hours before the final dress rehearsal Gemma's mother sends a team of hairstylists to school to put our hair in period-appropriate styles. We decided it would be most fun to dress in early-1920s style for the whole performance. We sit backstage in the dressing room while our silky locks are pulled, teased, and pinned according to the vintage *Vogue* photos that Gemma has chosen. The guys have their hair oiled and slicked, making them look surprisingly handsome, even Rhys—I can momentarily forget that he's a dork in his tweed suit, except when he tries to imitate the melancholy look in the photo featuring Edward VIII, the king who abdicated the throne for an American divorcée.

"Gems, I could totally pass for a royal, right?" Rhys asks with exaggerated received pronunciation, like they use in *The Crown*.

"Definitely not posh enough," Gemma says, her face deadpan.

I can't tell if she's joking or not, but Rhys's downcast puppy-dog eyes make me burst out laughing. I feel a tug on my hair as the stylist tells me to stop moving.

When our hair is done, a team of makeup artists comes and starts lining, blushing, and powdering us—even the boys. Snowy tells a reluctant Rhys that it's normal in the theater for everyone to wear makeup. "So your eyes pop on stage," she says.

Rainbow is as new to wearing makeup as I am, and

we giggle and blow kisses to each other with our ruby-red lips. Gemma tells us we need to be more serious.

When we're perfectly primped, Gemma lines us all up and looks us up and down, as if we were undergoing some sort of military inspection. She stops at me and does a double take. I brace myself for some critique of my appearance.

"Holly-Mei, I forgot to mention it earlier, but your eyebrows look nice."

"Oh, really? Millie helped me."

"Well, it looks professionally done."

"Um, thanks." I hold my head up a little higher. Wow, Gemma-approved eyebrows. I feel like we've turned a corner.

During this final dress rehearsal, we get to watch all the other groups perform. Our group is scheduled to go last. Rosie's group is electric: a rhythmic combination of the beat of Cantopop and moves that wouldn't be out of place in a Blackpink video. I can't see her on stage, though; I hope everything's okay. Then suddenly, when the music slows, she appears barefoot in a flowy white dress that makes her look like an angel when she spins. She jumps through the air, and the dancers catch her. They finish with an elaborate sequence to drumbeats that boom like thunder. I jump out of my seat and clap when they're done. Henry joins me in standing, as does the rest of the grade. He puts two fingers in his mouth and whistles while I shout *Woo-hoo!*

"She's really amazing, isn't she?" he says, beaming. Her face looks the same when she talks about him. I wonder if it means they are going to be hanging out more, just the two of them.

Straight after, we break for intermission, and I see Gemma rush out of the auditorium. I follow her to the bathroom to make sure she's okay.

"Don't be nervous. You'll be amazing," I say when I catch up to her.

"I hope so." She gives me a weak smile. "I just didn't expect any other group to be as good."

"There's room for both our groups to shine," I say gently.

"Maybe you're right."

As we are about to leave, she gives herself one more look in the mirror. "You know what? I'm going to get the necklace and put it on now, so all the other students can see it."

"Why don't we wait for the actual performance to-morrow?"

"No need to wait. We'll wow the others today, and then tomorrow we'll wow the parents."

"Okay. I'll come with you." I still don't get why she's so needy and determined to be the center of attention.

We walk in silence to her locker, and as she fiddles with her combination, I look at my reflection in a classroom window and tug at my collar. Suddenly, I hear a sharp shriek beside me. Gemma stands in front of her open locker.

"It's gone! Oh my God."

I walk over and peer into the locker. "It's probably under your bag."

"No, I looked." She starts emptying her locker contents onto the floor—bag, books, extra uniform, extra PE clothes, deodorant, perfume, mouthwash, a whole drugstore—but no hard briefcase with the necklace.

"Why was it even in your locker? Shouldn't it have been somewhere safer?" I regret it as soon as it comes out of my mouth, knowing how I sound like such an adult, and it's not helping.

"I locked it!" Gemma wails.

"Does anyone know your combination?"

"I don't know. I changed it to 8-8-8, my lucky number."

"That's everyone's lucky number," I say, surprised and a touch condescending. Eight is the luckiest number in Chinese, because the word for *eight*, ba, sounds like fa, which means *to become rich.*

"But no one steals here," she continues to wail. "I thought it was safe."

"Weren't Theo's parents supposed to bring it tomorrow night?"

"I made him bring it early so I could try it on with my hair up, in case I had to change the style to suit the necklace." Gemma gives out a little sob and dabs her eyes expertly so her makeup doesn't run. "Let's go tell Ms. Salonga and school security."

"No, wait. We can fix this on our own. If we tell someone, it'll put a spotlight on us." It will make my mom look bad.

"We really should tell a teacher," says Gemma, unconvinced.

"No, trust me. We can fix this our way. Isn't your mother the chair of the PTA? This will definitely make her look bad."

"I hadn't thought of that."

Just then, Rainbow appears at the end of the hallway.

"Shhh, we need to keep quiet," I whisper.

"Maybe you're right."

"I am right." It can't be worse than her idea to leave a priceless treasure in her locker.

"Guys!" Rainbow calls, waving her arms frantically. "We're on in five minutes, let's go. We were looking everywhere for you. I thought maybe you came to get the necklace."

"Nah, we decided to wait for the real show tomorrow for the big reveal," I say.

As we walk back toward the auditorium, I confidently whisper to Gemma, "I think I know who did this." I'm so disappointed to be thinking this of my new friend. He seems like such a good guy. But he's the one person I know who has it in for us, for Theo in particular. The thief can be none other than Devinder Singh.

19

The heavy red velvet curtain falls at the conclusion of our dress rehearsal. Backstage, I avoid looking at Theo, afraid that if I meet his eyes, I'm going to blurt out the news about the necklace. Plus, I don't want to see his dimples. It'll just make me feel guiltier for keeping this dilemma from him.

Gemma motions her head toward the exit sign. I grab my new purse, a treat from Auntie Helen on our Shenzhen trip, and we slink out of the auditorium and regroup in the stairwell. She sits on the steps, her hands red from all the wringing, and looks up at me with expectant eyes.

"I know where to look," I say.

"You really think Dev would do this?"

"You heard him the other day when Theo brought out the necklace. He's still bitter about the science fair." Although, I have to say I'm disappointed after all my efforts to get him and Theo to make up. I honestly thought he would try. "Come on, let's go."

We turn toward the lobby of the new wing. The various groups are adding final touches to their projects for the exhibition—art installations, graphic posters, photo collages. We hide behind a marble column and watch a group of people readjust the positioning of framed black-and-white photos under a banner that reads *Indian Diaspora in Hong Kong: Then and Now*. It looks fascinating, but I'm not here for a history lesson. I wait for a minute, then I see him, hands full. Dev Singh looks likely to be busy for some time.

I grab Gemma's hand, and we run toward the upper-school lockers. Dev's locker is easy to pick out. It's got a small TK-branded sticker on it, with its logo of two elephants crossing trunks as if they were field hockey sticks.

"Keep a lookout for anyone coming," I say.

In my mind, I go through the myriad of lock combinations he could have. Would he also have changed his to lucky 8-8-8? Has he ever told me his favorite number?

What am I going to do if I can't figure it out? I grab the lock, and before I desperately try random sets of numbers, I give the lock a little tug. Wonder of wonders, it's not even closed! I know Rosie never locks her locker; she says it's too much of a bother to fiddle with the combination between classes. I turn the padlock over and look both ways down the hall before I slide it off the latch. Even though the metal is cold, it feels like a hot potato in my hand. The locker door creaks open, and my eyes dart around inside, scanning the contents. There's nothing except a math textbook, an apple, and a pair of PE shorts. I slam the locker shut.

"Find anything?" Gemma asks.

"No, but I know another place to look. The field hockey equipment storage hut. Dev keeps his hockey bag there because It's too big for the locker." And it's big enough to easily hide a hard-shelled jewelry case.

We walk outside past the empty playing field and to the single-story brick building behind some bushes. It looks old, like it's been here since the school opened eighty-eight years ago. The paint around the door frame is peeling, and the hinges are rusted. I grab the knob. The door is locked.

245

"Do you have a key?" Gemma asks.

"No, but I don't think we need one. Look." The knob rattles under my grip. I open my purse and grab something to stick inside the shank.

"Why do you have tweezers in your purse?"

"In case I needed to touch up my eyebrows," I say with a laugh as I twist and turn the tweezers.

"You look like you've done this before. Burgle much?"

"No, I just forget my keys once in a while. We had a similar lock in the garage back home." I hear a soft clack from inside the knob, and it turns easily in my hand. "Voilà!" I say as I step into the hut.

I pull my phone out of my purse and flick on the flashlight function to search for the light switch.

"Over there. Pull the string," Gemma says.

A lone, naked bulb lights up the interior. The walls are lined with shelves filled with goalie bags, sticks, cones, and boxes full of pinnies. The air is heavy and damp, like an underground cellar.

"This place smells." Gemma wrinkles her nose. "Like PE kit that's never been washed."

"Probably because it never has," I say. "Here are the hockey bags." I walk to the end of the hut where a dozen stick bags stand on end and rummage through until I find the one with Dev's name on it. Bingo. I pull it out and lay it flat on the ground. I pass Gemma my phone and tell her to give me more light. I don't want to miss opening any zippers. I go through each compartment one by one, but I find nothing besides shin pads, extra socks, and turf shoes.

I sit back on my heels and let out a long breath, just as the light on my phone goes off.

"Well?" Gemma asks.

I slowly place the items back in the bag and put it back where I found it.

"Nothing."

"You said you were certain."

"I was. But I guess I was wrong." Disappointment tinged with relief surges through me. I'm so happy I was wrong about Dev.

"Well, I'm going to find Ms. Salonga to tell her what happened. Are you coming?"

"Yes, sure," I say as I trudge behind her, pulling the cord to shut the light on my way to the door.

"Hey, it's too dark," Gemma says.

"Well, turn my phone light back on."

"I can't, your phone's out of battery."

Great. This night can't get any worse. There's no moon out, but at least the school security lamp shines through the skylight and illuminates the way to the door.

"Oh. My. God," Gemma says in a panicked voice.

"What now?" I don't need any more drama.

"The door. It won't open." She continues to fiddle with the knob.

"Move over," I say. I'm sure it just needs some muscle. I turn the knob, but it spins and spins around in my hand. "Shoot. Can you text Rainbow or Rhys to come find us?"

"I don't have my phone," Gemma says, her voice screeching.

I freeze. My phone is dead, the door is broken, and we are somewhere no one is going to find us. I pound on the door and start yelling, hoping someone will hear us, but after a minute, my throat and my fists hurt, and I know no one will come. I put my head on the door and bang it softly but rhythmically, as I try to drown out the panicked wails from Gemma beside me.

"This is all your fault, Holly-Mei Jones. If you had listened to me in the first place, we wouldn't be here."

"I was just trying to help," I say softly.

"Well, is there anything else in that fake purse of yours

248

that might be useful?" Gemma asks in full condescending mode.

"Right, we're in a huge pile of crap right now, and all you can think to do is make fun of my purse? You're so spoiled!" I let out a huge huff.

"What?" She sounds incredulous.

"You think you can have whatever you want."

"You don't know what you're talking about."

"Don't I? Isn't our grade doing the exhibition because your parents have a wing named after them? A school wing! Your life is so easy."

"My life is not easy."

I let out a little scoff.

"You don't know anything, Holly-Mei," she says as she crumples to the floor. "If I don't do well tomorrow, they're going to send me away. Far away. Just like Justin." Gemma's last words come out almost inaudibly.

I sit down beside her. "Who's going to send you away? Who's Justin?"

"My parents are going to send me away. Justin's my brother. He's at boarding school in Connecticut, and he hates it. He cried his whole first year and kept begging to come home, but my parents said it was good for him, that it would toughen him up. That we're too coddled. And they told me that they think it'll be good for me, too. They're even making me do practice exams and mock interviews with some education consultant," says Gemma. She puts her head in her hands. "But if I do well on this and make them proud, make them look good, maybe they'll let me stay." Her voice squeaks, and my heart tears at the sound.

"Is that why you were in Canada?" I ask, wondering if this is why she was being so cagey about being on my flight.

Gemma nods. "They're having me visit schools all over the world. I don't want to go to any of them."

I lift my arm as high as my dress allows and put it around her. I guess not everything is as it seems. Her life looks so easy. So perfect. But maybe not everything that sparkles is gold.

"I'm sorry. For what your parents want to do. And for dragging you on this hopeless chase. I was just so desperate to fix it. I don't know what I was thinking."

"I know you were trying to help."

I'm surprised she says this, and it gives me courage to say more.

"Helping would have been listening to your plan to tell someone. I've just messed things up for the both of us." We sit in silence for a few seconds before she speaks.

"I messed things up first. I was the one that insisted that Theo bring the necklace today. And the video with the macaron cheeks—that was so mean of me."

"It was pretty mean." I give a dry laugh. "Why did you do it?"

"I saw you becoming friends with Theo," she says.

"And?" I turn to face her.

"And… I wanted to make sure he wouldn't stop being my friend, too," she says meekly, like she's embarrassed.

I give her a gentle knock with my arm. "Friendships can be shared. There's always some to go around."

"Do you think you have enough friendship for me?"

"Definitely." I take her hand in mine as we sit in the damp and dark shed together. The heaviness of our situation suddenly feels a bit lighter.

20

Gemma and I pass the time raiding the hockey team's stash of supplies. We try the various flavors of energy bars (chocolate-peanut butter is deemed the favorite) and wash them down with bottles of Pocari sports drink. I have no idea how much time goes by before we hear the sound of voices outside the equipment-hut door. Enough time for our coiffed hair to have become a mess and our dresses to have got wrinkled and dirty from sitting on the floor.

"In here!" Gemma and I both yell and bang on the door.

We can hear some jangling and then someone mumbles about a broken lock. "Stand back!" a voice tells us, and a few seconds later there is a huge clang of metal on metal. A uniformed security guard, a wrench in one hand and a flashlight in the other, bursts through the door.

"Sir, they are here," he says.

"Thank God." It's Mr. Gregg. He steps in and wipes the sweat from his forehead. "Are you girls both safe and unharmed?"

Gemma and I both nod.

"It's almost midnight. What are you doing in here?" He sounds more annoyed than concerned.

"It's my fault, Mr. Gregg. I made Gemma come and look for something. But then we couldn't open the door."

"We came together," Gemma says, looking at me and nodding.

"The lock has been tampered with from the outside," the security guard says.

So getting locked in is my fault, too. "That's my doing also, Mr. Gregg." He glares at me. I look at Gemma and hope my eyes convey how sorry I am. She mouths *It's okay* to me.

He marches us back to the lobby and tells us our parents are on their way.

"Gemma, your mother called me when your driver couldn't find you. Security has been searching the school inside out. Girls, both of your parents are beside themselves with worry."

"Sorry again," I mumble.

"How irresponsible of you!" he says, looking directly at me. "Miss Jones, due to your behavior tonight, I've decided you won't be allowed to participate in the gala tomorrow."

"It's not all her fault," Gemma starts to argue.

"She just told me it was."

"But—" she tries again.

"It's late. I should be back in my own comfortable home, and I'm here fixing her mess." He gestures to the bench by the front doors. "Wait here. Your parents should be here shortly," he says and stomps into the main office.

I put my hand on her shoulder. "It's no use. Concentrate on getting the necklace back."

If I hadn't been so stubborn, trying to force a quick fix so everything could be perfect, we wouldn't have wasted hours, and security might have already found the necklace and the real culprit. Maybe the group is better off without me.

It's only Dad that comes to get me. He gives me a big hug and tells me that he's so happy that we're safe. I'm silent on the drive home. My body and my mind are exhausted. Dad doesn't push it and just squeezes my hand to let me know he's there for me.

As soon as I step in the front door, I see Mom pacing in the living room, and I steel myself for her reaction.

"Follow me," she says and leads me to my room. She motions for me to sit on my bed, which I do without argument.

She sits down beside me, gets up, then sits down again. I can tell she is trying hard to control her voice as says, "Holly-Mei Jones, what were you thinking?"

"I was thinking I could fix everything." I tell her about the necklace going missing, my suspicions of Dev, and getting locked in the storage hut. And also about getting banned from the gala tomorrow.

"Why wouldn't you go straight for help?"

"Because I didn't want to risk bringing attention to the group. Let others know that we were in trouble."

"Why ever not?" Mom asks, sounding exasperated.

"Because I didn't want you to look bad," I say in an almost-whisper. I look tentatively up at her face. Mom furrows her brow.

"Why would you worry about that?" she asks, her tone suddenly gentle.

"Because of how I embarrassed you at Gemma's party. And because all those important people will be there tomorrow night. I just didn't want to mess things up for you again. You know, protect your new job."

"Oh, honey," she says as she takes my hand into hers. "Doing well in my job is my responsibility and mine alone. It's nothing you should worry about." Mom pulls me into a tight hug. I feel so safe in her arms.

"But you kept talking about important people, connections, guanxi. I don't want you to lose face again."

"I shouldn't have put that kind of pressure on you. What really matters is being respectful and courteous and kind. That's the kind of behavior I want to see, expect to see, from you and your sister. I'm so sorry about the other stuff."

"Really?" I ask, looking up at her. She hugs me again.

"You and your sister are both going to fall down. You're going to make mistakes, but you'll learn from them. And don't forget your father and I are here to help you pick up the pieces and stand up again." She shakes her head. "Maybe I should have reminded you that supporting you is my job, not the other way around."

"No, Mom, we're supposed to support each other."

She smooths the hair out of my face. "You're right. Look at you, all grown-up and responsible, giving me a lesson. Let's both promise to do better."

"Promise." I pause before asking, "So you're not mad or disappointed that I won't be in the gala exhibition?"

"Get a good night's sleep, and we'll talk to Mr. Gregg tomorrow." She pats my leg and gets up from the bed.

"One more thing, Mom," I say. "Does this mean I can try out for the field hockey team?"

Mom shakes her head and laughs. "You crack me up, Holly-Mei."

"Is that a *yes*?"

"Fine. Yes, honey, it's a *yes*." And she bends down to give me a gentle kiss on the forehead.

21

I wake up to the sound of the doorbell ringing. I roll over to fall back asleep, but soon there is a gentle knock on my bedroom door.

"Poppet, you have a visitor."

"Who is it?" I mumble.

"A young chap named Theo."

I bolt up, and my mind races. "Tell him I need a minute." I jump out of bed straight into the bathroom to brush my teeth and my hair, then I comb through my drawers for something to change into. What do you wear when you are about to be confronted by someone who just lost a family heirloom?

I move hesitantly into the living room, where Theo

is waiting for me on the sofa. He stands up when I walk toward him, and he looks agitated. His hand is tightly wrapped around a ball cap.

"Holly-Mei, about the necklace—" he starts.

I interrupt him. "I'm so sorry. Your parents must be freaking out. Are the police on the case?"

"No and no," he says.

"I don't understand."

"The necklace. It's safe."

"Oh, thank God." I flop down on the sofa, relaxing for the first time in hours. But why is Theo looking so unnerved? "What's wrong? Why are you here?"

He sits down beside me and takes a deep breath. "I took it."

"Took what? Took the necklace?" I must have heard incorrectly.

"Yes," he says. "I'm terribly sorry. I didn't know that you were looking for it, or that you even realized it was missing."

"What were you thinking, Theo? Do you know what you put me and Gemma through?" I try to control my voice so it sounds calm, but it cracks under the pressure.

"I know, I know. I'm sorry. I came to explain."

"Explain that you stole your own family's necklace?"

My forehead has so many creases in it from knitting and unknitting my eyebrows I could knit a sweater.

"I didn't mean to worry anyone. I just didn't want us to use it for the exhibition. I was angry, and I wasn't thinking. It was really stupid of me. Thoughtless."

"*Why* would you do that?"

"I was so mad at my father. Just before the dress rehearsal, he called to say that he wouldn't be able to make the gala. Urgent meeting in Singapore, and he'll be gone all weekend." He runs his fingers through his hair as if it's helping him clear his head. "I just didn't want to get up onstage and shine. I thought for once if I was just mediocre, my dad wouldn't have a chance to network. Networking makes him work even more." He looks at me, and I see his big brown eyes are all glasslike, as if he might cry. "I can't remember the last time we had a family meal," he says in a dejected voice.

"You need to tell him what you just told me. About wanting him around more." I think about how even though I'm super proud of Mom having a great career, I sometimes wonder if we would get along better if she weren't always so busy or stressed out. And then I feel guilty for thinking that because I know how hard she's worked to get where she is. I'm grateful Mom and I had that talk last night.

"Maybe," Theo continues. "But that's not the only reason I did it." He looks embarrassed. "I didn't want any more glory. Dev was right. I took all the credit onstage for the Science Cup when it didn't rightfully belong to me. My dad is always telling me how important it is to respect elders and save face, so when Mr. Gregg made a mistake in front of the whole school, including all the parents, I completely froze. I should have corrected him. But I didn't, and now I have lost a friend."

"You need to talk to Dev. Work things out. I'm sure he'd be open to listening to your explanation," I say encouragingly. I need to apologize to Dev, too, for ever thinking he would sabotage our group.

"I've been too embarrassed to bring it up with him."

"You both have some communication issues. Just sit down and talk. That's all it takes."

"You think?"

"For sure. And you guys are going to do great tonight."

"What do you mean *you guys*? You're in the group, too."

I tell him that Mr. Gregg banned me because of all the trouble I caused yesterday, and he shakes his head in disbelief. "This is my problem to fix. I won't freeze this time."

We stand backstage in a group huddle. Our hair and makeup done, and my dress like new, thanks to Joy's patience and care with a steam iron.

"Remember, this performance isn't a competition. It's a celebration. And we're going to do great, not because of some necklace, even though it *is* gorgeous—" I look over at Gemma, who flashes me a smile "—but because we worked hard and are telling a really amazing and moving story."

We put our hands in together. "Let's go and smash this," Theo says.

We walk confidently onstage and wait for the curtain to rise.

22

Rainbow and Snowy were right. At the end of our performance, the crowd is on their feet, the applause thunderous. I even hear a few bravos. The clapping doesn't
stop, so we glance at each other, smile, and bow again.
Snowy even gets to do the curtsy she's been practicing
all month. I look over at Gemma. She and the jade necklace shimmer in the spotlight. Regardless of what hap-
pens with her and boarding school, her parents have got
to be proud of what she's done, what we've done. I wonder if my parents are proud. I look out into the audience,
trying to spot them, trying to see their reactions, but I
can't make anyone out from the stage. But it doesn't mat-

ter. This project has turned out to be way better than I thought it would.

Learned lots of new things. Check.

Managed to get myself out of awkward situations, even if they were of my own doing. Check, check.

Made some friends. Check, check, check.

Ms. Salonga directs the entire Grade 7 class, all lucky eighty-eight of us, to the stage, and we take a bow. I see Rosie, still in her angelic organza dress, and I give her a gentle poke in the back. She turns around, and I whisper, "You were amazing." She mouths *You, too* back at me and puts her index finger and thumb together to form a heart. I put my finger and thumb together and flash her a heart back.

Mr. Gregg is beside himself as he sidles up to the podium microphone and gushes about our school, our generous donors, and of course, the namesake family of the new Tsien Wing. He calls Gemma and her parents to the front of the stage, and he presents each of them a giant bouquet of flowers so big that I'm surprised they don't lose their balance and tip over. Gemma's mother is beaming, and she waves to the crowd like she's the empress of Tai Tam Prep.

Mr. Gregg ends his speech with a bow, a mop of his forehead, and an invitation for everyone to head to the lobby for the unveiling of the portrait of Gemma's late grandfather, the patriarch of the Tsien family, and then up to the roof for food and drinks.

As soon as I step off the stage, I hear Millie squealing my name.

"That was so cool," she says, giving me a high five.

"Poppet, it was wonderful. Such wonderful family stories. I might just need to include that last one in my book." Dad cradles his belly as he laughs.

I look at Mom, still not a hundred percent sure what her reaction will be. She bites her lip. I wait for it. She starts to say something. "Holly-Mei…" But then she pauses. Instead, she pulls me into a hug. A nice, tight hug. And she whispers in my ear, "I'm so proud of you."

Up on the roof terrace, I leave Mom and Dad to mingle, and I go look for Rosie. I find her by the food table.

"Thank goodness that's over!" She piles her plate high with shrimp toast and chicken satay skewers. "I've been so nervous about my solo I haven't eaten all week."

"You were incredible," someone behind me says. It's

Gemma. She is still holding her ridiculously big bouquet, but she pulls out a long-stemmed red rose and passes it to Rosie.

"Thanks, Gemma. That means a lot."

As Henry comes up to congratulate Rosie, Gemma pulls out another rose from her ginormous bouquet and passes it to me. "Here's to starting our friendship fresh."

"To new friendships." I put my nose against the velvety petals and fill my senses with its sweet smell.

A few minutes later, the clouds part, and the silver sliver of a crescent moon appears. Things sure are looking brighter. Ah-ma was right about ku jin gan lai— *bitterness finishes, sweetness begins.* I thought I could leave home behind and forget about everyone, but I couldn't ever forget about Natalie. We've been texting everyday now.

The group makes plans to meet at the beach in Stanley tomorrow. I stay quiet: I don't want to assume I'm invited. But then Rainbow says, "You're coming, right?" and when I nod, all the others say, "Awesome." It feels pretty awesome, too.

I see Dev in the corner talking to a group of people.

When he makes a move toward the buffet, I beeline it over to him.

"Hey, Dev, I saw your photo exhibit. It was super interesting," I say as I load up my plate.

"Thanks. My family was really excited I decided to share the community's history."

"Your baby photo from Diwali was so cute. Those pointed shoes were the best," I gush.

"My jutti. I think my mom still has them." He laughs.

I gather my nerve and take a deep breath. "I have to confess something."

He looks at me expectantly.

"The necklace Gemma is wearing tonight. It went missing for a while yesterday. And I kind of thought you took it." I bite my lip waiting for the fallout.

"What?"

"I know, I was stupid, and I'm so sorry."

"Why would you think that?"

"I thought you wanted to get back at Theo. For the Science Cup drama. But I was totally wrong to think that."

Dev flicks his floppy hair out of his eyes and thinks for a few second. "It's forgotten."

"So—we're still friends?" I give him my best puppy-dog eyes.

"I'll just make you do some extra sprints around the pitch."

As we laugh, I notice Theo looking over at us. He looks like he wants to join, but is too nervous. I wave him over.

"Hey, Dev. Great photo display," Theo says.

"Thanks."

"I think you guys have a bunch of catching up to do," I add with a knowing nod toward Theo.

"I guess we do," says Dev, smiling.

Theo smiles back, dimples on show.

I slip away, leaving them to talk and patch things up.

As the party winds down, Snowy announces that it's picture time and directs the gala photographer to take our photo. All of us gather round—me, Rosie, Rainbow, Snowy, Gemma, Theo, Henry, Jinsae, and Rhys—arms around each other. Theo calls to Dev to join in, and he does. As the photographer counts down from three, we grin cheekily and flash our fingers up in a V as we say *Cheese.*

Back in bed, my phone pings. Snowy has sent the photo to our group chat. I stare at it for a few minutes, thinking about how I just met these people last month, but already feel like I've made real friends. And I may be far away from Canada, but this place is feeling a little like home with all the new family traditions, like FaceTiming with Ah-ma, making dumplings with Dad, hiking with cousins, even shopping with Millie. I forward the photo to Ah-ma and caption it: Gan lai.

* * * * *

AUTHOR'S NOTE

I could think of no better place to set the story of Holly-Mei Jones, a mixed Taiwanese Canadian who moves abroad for the first time, than the city of Hong Kong. My fourteen years in Hong Kong were magical and my experiences there have influenced everything I write. It is where I explored and fully embraced my Chinese heritage. I learned about foods, festivals, and folktales. I even learned to speak Mandarin (*hai ke yi*) and some Cantonese (*siu siu*). This book is my love letter to Hong Kong.

I grew up in Ottawa, Canada, a child of immigrants. My father, an only child, fled his home alone at the age of twenty-one during the Hungarian Revolution. My mother emigrated from Taiwan as a graduate student, along with many of her nine siblings. The Taiwanese side of my family, with over twenty cousins, was a huge part of my childhood. I thought it was normal for a whole family to spend their holiday in my aunt's sewing room on the floor in sleeping bags. At our gatherings, charades, volleyball, and tennis were always ultracompetitive.

My sister and I were the only mixed cousins and there were very few mixed-race kids in our community growing up. Luckily, I was rarely made to feel embarrassed by or self-conscious about my heritage. Outwardly, I was a typical suburban Canadian playing field hockey and soccer on the school team and hanging out with friends. At home, I had two distinct cultures to call my own, with their interesting histories, colorful customs, and delicious foods. Perhaps it was due to my large extended Taiwanese family and summers spent with the small local Hungarian community, but I have always loved being biracial. The only grief I received was from elders who complained that I couldn't speak either of my parents' languages.

The Not-So-Uniform Life of Holly-Mei is a story about kids doing regular kid things and facing typical adolescent dilemmas, but with characters that just happen to be Asian. Where heritage is part of the story, not the basis for it. I wanted readers to see mixed-race and Asian kids who are happy and confident in who they are. I also wanted to add to the growing collection of books that widen the lens of what a story with Asian characters can look like. After all—*Asians, they're just like us!*

I hope you enjoyed reading the book and following Holly-Mei's journey.

Christina

ACKNOWLEDGMENTS

I've often heard that writing a book is a solitary experience, but mine has been anything but. I am fortunate to have been surrounded by such a supportive network of publishing professionals, fellow writers, and good friends. A huge thank you to the following people:

Carrie Pestritto, my wonderful agent, who took a chance on me and helped me grow as a writer.

Rebecca Kuss, my editor, whose kind and steady hand teased out the best Holly-Mei story I could tell. You also showed me how important it is not only to have Own Voices in storytelling but also Own Voices in publishing.

Claire Stetzer and Bess Braswell at Inkyard Press: Your excitement for this book was infectious. Claire, a huge thank you for gently and patiently guiding me through the publishing process. Additional thanks to Yao Xiao, Erin Craig, Gigi Lau, and the Inkyard design team for the gorgeous cover and illustrations. And Heather Foy at HarperCollins: I'm so delighted to work with one of my oldest childhood friends.

Susan Blumberg-Kason, the best cheerleader ever. Your positivity was a ray of sunshine.

The Hong Kong University MFA Class of 2020. A tumultuous year of protests and COVID-19 only brought us closer together. Special thanks to those who stayed on for the writing group and continued to lift each other up: Mariella Candela, Fung Ying Cheng, Christy Hirai, Tom K. E. Chan, Kelly Chan, and especially to Gabrielle Tsui, Dr. Shivani Salil, and Jenny Ho Chang for reading the entire manuscript. And multiple thanks to Jenny for your skillful editing of multiple iterations!

The group at SCBWI Hong Kong for your support, guidance, and laughs over the last few years. In particular Rachel Ip, John Brennan, and Mio Debnam for helping me get my initial idea off the ground, and Ritu Hemnani and Erica Cohen Lyons for your middle-grade writing support.

The entire team at Bring Me A Book Hong Kong, especially Pia Wong, Su Lee Chen, Annie Ho, Rachel Ip, and Michelle Bang. You showed me how much difference quality books and reading aloud can make in children's lives.

The group of amazing, smart, and strong women I call my Core—your friendship and support mean the world to me. Ellie Poulton, Helen Dowding, Aisling Dwyer, Katy Spooner, and especially Katie Daly, whose keen book-loving eye has guided me from my initial idea, which I talked about for years, to this last draft. HKFC Field Hockey D-ream Team forever.

All the people I interviewed for this book, whose insights and anecdotes were so valuable to bringing the story to life. I call you my Youngspiration team: Dev Dillon, Mollie O'Neill, Jemma Abbs, Amelia McColl, Shira Kim, Sandy and Gemma Liang, Elena Valenzuela and Lizzie Farquhar, Amanda and Max Irvine, Simone and Chloe Matrundola, Alicia Freiin von Richthofen, Anne-Marie Kwan, Alma and Stella Erro, and Sophie, Kara, and Siena Poulton.

And thanks to those who helped in a myriad of other ways. Ken and Liz Chow, not only for your cherished friendship, but also for answering all my questions about local Hong Kong culture. Sandra Abi-Rashed for your boundless energy and marketing expertise. Andrea Fessler for chatting to me about parent perspectives while doing our weekly run on Bowen Road. Rachel Middagh for helping me inject warmth into my bio. Emma Rhoda for teaching me about low social thinking. Catherine Irvine and Robert Aldridge for your insights into school guidance departments. Tracy C. Gold for your editing help.

Finally to those at home and in my heart. My sister, Natalie, for inspiring the bond between Holly-Mei and Millie. To my parents, Ching Yue and Tibor, for filling my childhood with sweetness. To Analiza Evangelista and Kimberly Agasa-Nesperos for helping to take care of the house and kids so I could be free to write. To E & S, who are so proud to see Mommy's books on the shelf; and to Jukka, for your constant and very Finnish support: love you always.

GLOSSARY

Chinese and English are the official languages of Hong Kong. Cantonese is the predominant form of Chinese in the city. Mandarin, the official language of Mainland China, is now heard more frequently on the streets of Hong Kong and forms part of the local school curriculum. Cantonese and Mandarin words share the same traditional characters (used in Hong Kong and Taiwan, while Mainland China uses simplified characters), but have different pronunciation. Taiwanese is also a distinct language and is spoken widely on the island of Taiwan, particularly in the south, where my mother and her family are from.

Below are the Chinese words found in the book in traditional characters with their definitions. The words are in Mandarin Chinese, except where noted, and include the pinyin tone marks, which indicate the pitch of the word.

The same syllable pronounced with a different tone has a completely different meaning. Mandarin has four tones. For simplicity, only Mandarin tones are noted.

For example:
1st tone—ā:
the *a* is said in a steady, high pitch. As in 媽 mā *mother*

2nd tone—á:
the *a* is said in a rising pitch, like you are asking a question. As in 麻 má *linen*

3rd tone—ǎ:
the *a* is said in a dipping tone that falls and rises again. As in 馬 mǎ *horse*

4th tone—à:
the *a* is said with a sharp drop from high to low. As in 傌 mà *to scold*

SAYINGS

Baobei 寶貝 **bǎobèi** [bow (as in take a bow) bay]: *treasure, darling*

Meiyou wenti 沒有問題 **méiyǒu wèntí** [may yo when tea]: *no problem*

Hao ba 好吧 **hǎo ba** [how ba]:
fine (ba indicates reluctant approval to a suggestion)

Chi ku 吃苦 **chī kǔ** [chi (as in chip without the *p*) koo]:
swallow bitterness, endure hardship

Ku jin gan lai 苦盡甘來 **kǔ jìn gān lái** [koo gin gan lie]:
bitterness ends and sweetness begins

Yat, yi, sam, sei, ng 一, 二, 三, 四, 五 [yat, ee, sam, say, ing]:
Cantonese for 1, 2, 3, 4, 5

Mm goi 唔該 [mm goy (as in boy)]:
Cantonese for thank you, please, and excuse me

Guanxi 關係 **guānxi** [gwahn see]:
relationships, connections, network

PEOPLE

Ah-ma 阿嬤 [ah mah]:
*Taiwanese for grandmother, either father's mother or
mother's mother*

Ah-gong 阿公 [ah gong]:
*Taiwanese for grandfather, either father's father or
mother's father*

Maa maa 嫲嫲 [ma ma (with long a sounds)]:
Cantonese for father's mother

Po po 婆婆 [pahw pahw]:
Cantonese for mother's mother

FOOD

Jiaozi 餃子 **jiǎozi** [gee-ow ze]:
dumplings

Dan tat 蛋撻 [dan tat (with a soft second *t*)]:
Cantonese for egg custard tart

Har gau 蝦餃 [har gow (as in how)]:
Cantonese for shrimp dumplings

Char siu bao 叉燒包 [char see-you bow (as in take a bow)]:
Cantonese for barbecue pork bun

Cheung fan 腸粉 [chung fun]:
Cantonese for stuffed rice flour roll

Bolo bao 菠蘿包 [bo low bow (as in take a bow)]:
Cantonese for pineapple bun

Tang yuan 湯圓 **tāng yuán** [tahng you-en]:
a dessert of rice-flour dumplings in a sweet soup

AH-MA'S DUMPLINGS

This is the dumpling recipe that my mother, the real Ah-ma, used to make when I was a child. It's inspired from her favorite cookbook, *Pei Mei's Chinese Cook Book, Volume 1* by Fu Pei Mei, a Taiwanese chef with whom she took dumpling-making classes. I remember trying to help her close the dumplings, but I always ended up overfilling them, so that they burst open when boiled. The original recipe calls for homemade wrappers, but I've simplified it with store-bought wrappers, and it should make twenty-eight dumplings. Make sure to always have an adult with you in the kitchen.

INGREDIENTS

1 small can of bamboo shoots, chopped
340 g ground pork
120 g prawn (shrimp), chopped
3 stalks of green onion, chopped
1 tbsp of fresh ginger, chopped
2 tbsp soy sauce
2 tbsp sesame oil
½ tsp sugar
2 tsp sea salt
1 pack of dumpling wrappers

Yields 28 dumplings

1. Combine the bamboo shoots, pork, and prawn, and mix well. Stir in the rest of the ingredients.

2. Take a dumpling wrapper and spoon in one scoop into the middle. Put a touch of water on your finger and dab the edge of the wrapper before folding, to help it stick. Close the wrapper in half, pinching at the center, and continue pinching along the edge. Bring the two edges of the semicircle together, like the dumpling is giving itself a hug, and it can stand up in a pan.

3. To cook, either boil or pan fry.

   BOILING: Heat a pot full of water with 1 tsp of salt. Add 14 dumplings and reduce the heat to medium, while keeping at a boil. Cook for 3 to 5 minutes until the dumplings float to the surface. Remove and repeat with the next 14.

   PAN FRY: Add 2 tbsp of vegetable oil to a frying pan. When the oil is heated, put in 14 dumplings, and cook for 1 to 2 minutes. When the bottoms of the dumplings are golden brown, add in ½ cup of hot water from a kettle, and cover for 2 to 3 minutes. Once the water is absorbed, uncover and let the dumplings fry gently for another minute before serving. Repeat with the next 14.

4. Serve with dipping sauce. Ideally a 1:1 mix of soy sauce and Worcestershire sauce, with a touch of shredded ginger.

MILLIE'S RED BEAN CREAMSICLES

A creamy and lightly sweetened treat to have on hot summer days. Easy to make, easy to love.

INGREDIENTS

*100 g canned red beans or red bean paste
(adzuki beans, not kidney beans)**
300 ml whole milk
125 ml condensed milk

1. If using canned beans, strain and rinse them. If using paste, please go straight to the next step.

2. Blend all the ingredients together in a blender or with a hand mixer. Or use a whisk and some arm muscle.

3. Pour into Popsicle molds.**

4. Freeze for at least 6 hours.

5. Run the mold under warm water to help loosen the Popsicle. Enjoy!

*If you can't find canned red beans or red bean paste, you can buy dry adzuki beans. Take ½ cup and soak for 3 hours. Strain and add 2 cups of water and simmer on low heat for 60 minutes. Drain and then go to step 2.

**If you don't have a Popsicle mold, you can use plastic cups, an ice cube or muffin tray, or an old yogurt cup, with a plastic spoon or wooden Popsicle stick as a handle.

Makes approximately 6 Popsicles